by Henry Winkler and Lin Oliver

HANK ZIPZER

The World's Greatest Underachiever

Grosset & Dunlap • New York

J
WIN

24.00

*For Debra Dorfman—for your positive, supportive guidance and
leadership, and oh ... for saying yes.
And always, always to my Stacey.—H.W.*

*For Cole Baker—my favorite
cooking companion and cherished
third son—with love.—L.O.*

Visit us at www.abdopub.com

Library bound edition © 2006

Spotlight, a division of ABDO Publishing Company Inc., is a distributor of high quality
reinforced library bound editions for schools and libraries.

Text copyright © 2004 by Fair Dinkum and Lin Oliver Productions, Inc. Illustrations copyright
© 2004 by Grosset & Dunlap. All rights reserved. Published by Grosset & Dunlap, a division
of Penguin Young Readers Group, 345 Hudson Street, New York, New York 10014.
GROSSET & DUNLAP is a trademark of Penguin Group (USA) Inc. Printed in the U.S.A.

Library of Congress Cataloging-in-Publication Data

Winkler, Henry, 1945-
    Holy enchilada! / Henry Winkler and Lin Oliver.
        p. cm.—(Hank Zipzer, the world's greatest underachiever)
    Summary: Efforts to impress a visiting student from Japan cause Hank to hide his dyslexia while the
gang makes enchiladas for a Multi-Cultural Day lunch, and Hank is afraid he was very wrong about
the amount of chili powder called for in the recipe.
    ISBN 0-448-43353-2 (pbk.)—0-448-43554-3 (hardcover)—1-59961-105-8 (Reinforced Library
Bound Edition)
    [1. Schools—Fiction. 2. Japanese—Fiction. 3. Cookery, Mexican—Fiction. 4. Learning disabili-
ties—Fiction. 5. Multiculturalism—Fiction. 6. Humorous stories.] I. Oliver, Lin. II. Title. III. Series.

PZ7.W72934 Ho 2004
[Fic]—d22

2004009671

All Spotlight books are reinforced library binding and manufactured in the United States of America.

CHAPTER 1

"ITCHY KNEE," Ms. Adolf said, staring at me like I knew what on earth she was talking about.

Ms. Adolf stood there next to my desk, tapping her foot impatiently. Squinty gray eyes peeped out from behind her gray glasses. I could tell she wanted me to say something, but my mind was totally blank.

"What comes next, Henry?" she asked.

What do you say after itchy knee? Rashy ankle? Scratchy elbow?

I wasn't in the mood for riddles. My head was still spinning from the math test I had just taken.

We had just finished our Unit Four math test on fractions, and I don't mind telling you, it was the most confusing test I had ever taken. To begin with, math isn't my idea of fun. And tests, unit or otherwise, definitely don't make it onto my top ten list of "Things to Look Forward to on a Monday Morning." I guess if I were like our class genius, Heather Payne, who has never gotten anything lower than an A on any test, I might have a different opinion of tests. But when your highest grade ever on a math test is a D-plus—well, that kind of sucks any possible fun right out of the picture.

And fractions—who invented them, anyway? Probably the same guy who invented decimal points. I don't get the point of either fractions or decimal points.

I don't get the point of decimal points. Hey, that's not bad. Way to make yourself laugh, Hank Zipzer!

I must have spaced out for a second, enjoying my little joke, because suddenly I heard Ms. Adolf speaking to me.

"Henry," she barked. "Did you hear me? I said *itchy knee*. Do you know what comes after that?"

I looked down at my knee. Now that she brought it up, I noticed that it was itching a bit. But how could Ms. Adolf possibly know that? Oh, no! Maybe she had invented a secret itch-detector device and tucked it in the waist-band of her gray skirt. Maybe at this very minute she was scanning everyone in the class for mosquito bites or patches of itchy dry skin. Wow, that thought gave me the creeps. If there's one thing you don't want, it's your fourth-grade teacher secretly detecting your private skin conditions.

Ms. Adolf was still staring at me. Not so much staring as glaring, burning two holes into my forehead. She wasn't going to back down on this knee thing until I answered.

"Actually, I do have kind of an itchy knee," I finally said. "On a scale of one to ten, with one being 'no itch' and ten being 'it itches so bad that you have to scratch for an hour,' I'd say it itches three."

Everyone in the class burst out laughing.

"I can't believe you, Zipper Zit!" Nick McKelty howled from the row in back of me, blasting out a stream of his rotten-egg breath. "You are as dumb as a . . ."

I guess he couldn't come up with the end of that thought, because he suddenly stopped laughing and looked around the classroom in a panic. His eyes fell on a bulletin board with a poster of a gray whale. I could almost see his big, slow brain latching on to that poster.

"You're as dumb as a whale," McKelty said, looking real proud that he had finished his thought.

"That shows how much you know, McKelty," my best friend Frankie Townsend shot back at him. "Whales are extremely intelligent life-forms."

"Unlike you, Nick," my other best friend Ashley Wong chimed in.

Ashley and Frankie live in my apartment building and we hang out together all the time. We've been best friends since preschool. Trust me, no one can say something mean to one of us without hearing from the other two.

Ms. Adolf clapped her hands three times, which she does when we're talking out of turn without raising our hands. If you talk after that, you get sent to Principal Love's office for one of his boring lectures about how great it is to have self-control, because without it, you'll spin into outer space. No one wanted to visit Principal Love, so we all shut up fast.

"I wasn't saying itchy knee, Henry," Ms. Adolf said, turning back to me. "I was saying *ee-chee, nee*. That's counting in Japanese. *Ee-chee* is 'one,' and *nee* is 'two.' "

Why didn't she just say that at the beginning? How was I supposed to know she was spewing Japanese? Do I look like I live in Tokyo?

"Does anyone know what comes after *ee-chee, nee?*" she asked.

"Why don't you ask Ashley Wong?" McKelty hollered out. "I'll bet she speaks Japanese."

Ashley pushed her glasses up on her nose and started twirling her ponytail, like she does when she's mad.

"For your information, I'm not Japanese," she said. "My parents are from China. And here's some breaking news for you, McKelty. Japan and China are two entirely different countries."

"No reason to get so steamed up about it," McKelty muttered.

I thought Ashley was going to wind up and smash her fist into McKelty's arm, but Ms. Adolf clapped her hands three times again.

"Pupils," she said. "This is a very good introduction to our topic. This week we are celebrating Multi-Cultural Day. Everyone in school is going to be learning about people in other countries. Our class is going to be cooking foods from around the world for the special banquet lunch."

Katie Sperling raised her hand and shook it like she had to go to the bathroom.

"Yes, Katie," Ms. Adolf said.

"I hear people in France eat snails," said Katie.

"That's so gross," groaned Kim Paulson.

"I've eaten a snail," piped up Luke Whitman, whose nickname in our class is Captain Disgusto. "I liked the slimy part, but I spit out the antennae."

"Eeuuuwww," Katie and Kim both moaned at once. "There should be a law against Luke."

You've got to hand it to Luke, though. He's the only kid I know who would tell the two prettiest girls in the fourth grade that he spits out snail antennae.

Ms. Adolf just ignored Luke, like she usually does.

"To celebrate Multi-Cultural Day, we have a special treat in store for us," she went on. I think she actually smiled a little bit, showing a few of her upper teeth. They were the only thing about her that wasn't gray, but they were on the way to being yellow. "Our classroom is having a visitor from Japan. He's in the fourth grade, and his name is Yoshi Morimoto."

A visitor. That sounded interesting. At least, it sounded much more interesting than the stuff Ms. Adolf usually talks about, like spelling and fractions and note-taking skills.

"Yoshi's father, Mr. Morimoto, is the principal of our sister school in Tokyo," Ms. Adolf explained.

I wasn't sure what a sister school was, but I sure hoped it wasn't anything like my sister, Emily. She sleeps with her eyes open and flosses her teeth at the dinner table. I wondered if anything that gross went on at our sister school in Tokyo.

"Mr. Morimoto is touring schools in the United States," Ms. Adolf went on. "He's bringing his son, and they're coming to spend two days with us at PS 87."

"Can I introduce him to my tarantula, Mel?" Luke Whitman asked.

"Absolutely most certainly not!" Ms. Adolf answered.

I could see Frankie trying not to laugh. I knew that he was remembering the exact same thing I was. Once, Luke had brought Mel to class for Pet Day. Mel escaped from his cage and climbed up Ms. Adolf's leg. She screamed so loud, you could actually see her tonsils flopping around in the back of her throat.

"To make this visit very special, Mr. Morimoto has agreed to let his son Yoshi sleep over at the home of one of our students," Ms. Adolf went on. "He wants him to see how a typical fourth-grader in New York lives. We will be picking one of your families to host Yoshi."

My ears perked up like my dog Cheerio's do when he hears my dad's favorite opera singers screeching on TV.

I hope they pick my family. That would be so cool.

I love having guests from other countries. Well, to be honest, I've only had one. Vlady—

he's the sandwich-maker in my mom's deli—
spent a week with us when he first moved to
New York from Russia and was looking for an
apartment. We had a great time. He stayed up
really late with us, singing this wild Russian
song called "Kalinka Malinka" and telling us
stories about a circus bear named Igor who
followed him to school.

The only bad part was when Vlady brought
us a jar of caviar to eat. In case you don't know,
caviar is fish eggs. Most of the time, they're
bluish-black. They're supposed to be a treat, but
how can something that smells so, well, fishy be
a treat? When I thought Vlady wasn't looking, I
slipped my caviar to our dachshund, Cheerio.
When Cheerio thought I wasn't looking, he
pushed it out our tenth-floor window with his
nose. It landed plop on Mrs. Park's air-
conditioning unit. It stayed there for three days
until a pigeon came by and gobbled it up. Bye-
bye, fish eggs.

"If you would like to volunteer to host Yoshi,
please raise your hand now," Ms. Adolf said.

My hand shot up like a rocket. So did thirty-
two others'! In fact, the only person who didn't

raise his hand right away was Luke Whitman, and that's because his finger was too far up his nose to get it out in time.

Even though everyone else in the class was volunteering, I thought Ms. Adolf should pick me. After all, if things got dull, Yoshi and I could sit around and count to two in Japanese. I could do that, no problem.

Itchy knee.

CHAPTER 2

WE ALL DECIDED THAT THE ONLY FAIR WAY to pick who was going to host Yoshi was to pull a name out of a hat. After recess, Ms. Adolf told each of us to write our name down on a slip of paper. I thought we should put them in my Mets baseball hat, but some of the girls objected because I had gotten it pretty sweaty at recess. So instead we put the names in Ashley's lavender baseball cap, the one she decorated with a red rhinestone flower and a yellow stem.

Ms. Adolf closed her eyes, reached in, and pulled out one of the slips of paper. Here's what it said:

HANK ZIPZER.

Can you believe it?

In case you hadn't realized it, that's me!

CHAPTER 3

I WAS VERY EXCITED to have been chosen to host Yoshi. I still had to get permission from my parents before it was totally official. I was pretty sure I could get them to agree if I told them it was an educational experience. They're very big on educational experiences.

"Where is Yoshi going to sleep?" Ashley asked me as we sat down at our usual table in the lunchroom.

"I call top bunk," Frankie said, just assuming that he was going to sleep over when Yoshi did. "We'll put the Yosh Man on the floor. People in Japan sleep on the floor all the time, you know."

"That's not going to work," I answered. "Katherine might sneak up on him in the night and lick him with that sandpaper tongue of hers." Katherine is my sister Emily's pet iguana, and trust me, you don't want her long, sticky tongue anywhere near any of your body parts.

I opened my lunch bag and groaned. My mom had packed me another one of her science experiment sandwiches. My mom owns a deli called the Crunchy Pickle, and she's trying to come up with a new low-carb high-fiber bagel to sell at the deli. Since I'm always the guinea pig for her weird food experiments, she had packed me a broccoli mushroom bagel for lunch. Hold the cream cheese, of course, because that might actually taste good. Instead, she had covered my greenish-brownish bagel with ground-up garbanzo beans and parsley in soy juice. It looked like the stuff that holds the bricks in our fireplace together.

"I'll trade you half of mine for half of yours," I offered Frankie. He had a peanut butter and banana on Wonder bread that my taste buds were screaming for.

Frankie reached out and poked at my bagel with his finger. It didn't move.

"I think it's dead," he said. "Or dying."

Frankie handed me half of his peanut butter Wonder. After all these years of being my best friend, he just assumes he's got to give me half of

13

his sandwich on the days when my mom is practicing her creative cooking.

"I hope your mom doesn't try to feed one of those bagels to Yoshi," Ashley said. "He'll go running back to Japan."

"Actually, that's not possible," said a nasal voice from behind us. "Japan is an island country consisting of four main islands and more than three thousand small islands surrounded by water. It's not possible to run to Japan. Actually, he would have to swim."

It was Robert Upchurch, third-grade pest and Ruler of the Land of the Know-It-Alls. He lives in the same apartment building as Frankie, Ashley, and me, and his goal in life is to be our best friend and my sister Emily's boyfriend. Our goal in life is to keep him as far away as possible.

"Anyone object if I join you?" Robert asked, putting his tray down next to Ashley before we could say yes, we all object a lot.

"Hey, Robert, my man," Frankie said, pushing my bagel over in front of his bony hands. "Why don't you try some of this delicious high-fiber bagel? It'll keep your jaws busy so you can't talk for a while."

Robert didn't get the insult, which is nothing new. Once when we were taking swimming lessons at the YMCA, a kid looked at Robert in his skinny little swimming trunks and said that he reminded him of a wet rat. Robert didn't feel bad. He just went off on a long rant about how a rat's skeleton can collapse to be thinner than a German pancake, which is why they're able to sneak under refrigerators to get forgotten bites of roast beef.

"Actually, fiber is excellent for the digestive system," Robert said, picking up the bagel and taking a major whiff of it. Robert is the kind of guy who smells everything before he eats it. "Fiber keeps your waste products moving through your bowels in a timely and healthy fashion."

"Robert," Ashley moaned. "Hasn't anyone ever told you that normal people don't talk about their bowels at the table?"

"I don't see what's wrong with it," Robert said. "Bowels carry human waste. Human waste is a completely normal product of the body."

"Yeah, so are boogers and dandruff flakes,

but we don't just blab on about them, dude," said Frankie.

Robert adjusted his tie and took a big bite of his fish taco. That's right. I said tie. Robert is the only kid I know who wears a tie to school. He is also the only kid I know who eats the fish tacos at our cafeteria.

I noticed that Ashley had stopped listening. She was staring at someone across the room.

"I don't believe my eyes," she whispered, pushing her plastic spoon into her lime Jell-O. "She's walking over here. To our table. I'm serious."

Frankie and I whipped around to see who Ashley was looking at. Yikes! It was Ms. Adolf. She was heading our way, carrying an overripe brown banana in a napkin.

No. This wasn't happening.

"Mind if I sit down next to you, Henry?" she asked.

Did I mind? Yes, I minded! I minded with every cell in my body, especially the ones that were going to be closest to her when she did sit down.

"Of course not," I said, hoping that maybe

I'd get lucky and she would sit down somewhere in New Jersey.

Everyone in the cafeteria had gotten quiet and was just staring at us. It's not natural for Ms. Adolf to cruise up to your table, throw a leg over the bench, and crank up a conversation. She's not exactly your warm and cuddly type of teacher.

"I'd like to talk with you about Yoshi," Ms. Adolf said, taking a bite of her banana. I noticed that she was eating the brown spot, the very spot that normal people cut off with a knife and throw in the garbage.

"What about him?" I asked.

"Well, Henry, I've been thinking. Don't you think Yoshi would like to see what life is like in a typical American family?"

"My family is going to blow him away," I said.

Ms. Adolf looked down at the table and saw my broccoli-mushroom bagel covered with garbanzo beans.

"I notice your mother's cooking is not exactly . . . uh . . . typical," she said, holding up the bagel, being careful to use the waxed paper it was lying on. "I wouldn't want it to frighten Yoshi."

She took another bite of her rotten banana. Boy, she should talk about scary food. I could see the rotten banana squishing between her teeth. It looked like the Yellow Blob in there.

"Zip's family is a little unusual, but they're totally fun," Frankie said. "Did you know they have a pet iguana?"

"Her name is Katherine," I said. "She sleeps in the bathtub."

"An iguana in the bathtub," Ms. Adolf said, raising her eyebrows so high, they almost shot off her forehead. "Is that good lavatory hygiene?"

I have to confess, I'm not crazy about Katherine myself, especially when I catch her hanging out in my underwear drawer. But I sure didn't like Ms. Adolf turning up her nose at our lavatory hygiene.

"Wait until Yoshi meets Cheerio," I said, trying to change the subject. "They'll get along great. He's the sweetest dog in the world. You've met him before."

"Oh, that dog!" Ms. Adolf said. "The one

that spins in circles until he knocks someone over. You know, Henry, that's not typical, either."

"It is for him," I said.

Frankie and Ashley cracked up, but Ms. Adolf just shook her head.

"Yoshi would love Hank's grandfather," Ashley said.

"Papa Pete is the best," Frankie added. "He'd make Yoshi an honorary grandkid, just like Ashley and me."

"I'm one, too," Robert said. "Even though Papa Pete is always complaining that I'm too skinny for him to pinch."

"Your grandfather, the one who eats those pickles," Ms. Adolf said.

"He makes them himself," I said proudly. "Garlic dills are Papa Pete's specialty."

"I hate to say this, Henry, but I don't think Japanese people enjoy garlic dills," said Ms. Adolf.

"Then they haven't lived," I answered.

"Henry," Ms. Adolf said, getting close enough to me so I could see the banana gunk between her teeth. "My point is that I think we

19

should put our best foot forward for our Japanese friends. And I'm not sure staying with your family will do that."

"Yoshi will have a great time at my house," I said to Ms. Adolf. I didn't know whether to be angry or sad, so I was both.

"Yeah," said Frankie. "Hank's family is cool. And warm. At the same time. Tell her, Ashweena."

"They're really thoughtful," added Ashley.

"Besides, America is a land of diversity," said Robert to Ms. Adolf. "Hank's family is diverse. Yes, indeed. Very, very, very, very diverse."

Ms. Adolf sighed. That shut her up once and for all. There was nothing she could say to that. She picked up her banana peel and left.

Way to go, Robert Upchurch!!

We all reached over and slapped Robert on the back. Unfortunately, we were too enthusiastic and sent the poor little dude flying right into his plate of fish tacos.

CHAPTER 4

Dictionary

AFTER LUNCH, while the rest of the class worked on their maps of the rivers of North America, Ms. Adolf called me to her desk.

"Henry," she said. "I want you to make a list of ten things you plan to do with Yoshi while he's staying at your house."

"That's a great idea, Ms. Adolf," I said. "I've been thinking in my mind about all kinds of fun things we could do together."

"Good," she said. "I'll come by your desk and check your list. And remember, Henry. Spelling counts."

Spelling counts? "Spelling counts" has to be my least favorite sentence in the English language. By the way, do you happen to know if it is a sentence? I don't have a clue.

Even though Ms. Adolf knows that I have learning challenges and that spelling is nearly impossible for me, she still grades me down if I make spelling mistakes. She says she thinks students with learning differences should have to learn just like everyone else. They just need to work harder at it. Obviously, she's never been inside my brain when it's trying to spell. Sometimes it's working so hard that you can almost smell the smoke. Finally, it just flops over and says, "I QUIT!"

But I wanted to have Yoshi at my house so much that I really worked at spelling every word on that list correctly. I even looked up a bunch of words in the dictionary, which is not easy for a kid with dyslexia, which is what I have.

At the beginning of the year, I couldn't use the dictionary at all. But I've been working with our school learning therapist, Dr. Lynn Berger, after school. She taught me how to sound out some words so I can look them up. When I do find a word in the dictionary, I feel really proud.

After I had checked every word I wasn't sure of in the dictionary, my list looked like this:

TEN FUN THINGS TO DO WITH YOSHI MORIMOTO
By Hank Zipzer
With a little help from Webster's Dictionary
(Okay, a lot of help)

1. Hang out in my room and play video games.
2. Hang out in Frankie's room and play video games.
3. Hang out in Ashley's room and play video games.
4. Watch monster movies on TV.
5. Watch ninja movies on TV.
6. Watch old episodes of *Happy Days* on TV.
7. Have a burping contest.
8. Have a burping contest while playing video games in my room.
9. Have a burping contest while watching *Happy Days* on TV.
10. Have a knuckle-cracking contest.

By the way, I spent almost an hour looking for the word "knuckle" in the dictionary. Did you know that there is a "k" at the beginning of that word? I swear to you, I don't know what it's doing there. It just sits there silently, waiting for you to start looking it up under "n." Luckily, Frankie is a really good speller and told me about that sneaky "k" so I could find the dumb word in the dictionary. Otherwise, our knuckle-cracking contest never would have made the list.

When I was finished with the list, I put my pencil down, sat back, and read it over. It sounded great to me. If I were Yoshi Morimoto and did everything on that list, I would go home thinking that America was the coolest, funniest country in the world.

When Ms. Adolf came over to check my list, I thought her eyes were going to zing out of her head and bounce all over the room like pinballs.

"Henry," she said, her neck getting all blotchy with those red spots that show up when she's really mad. "I hope this is a joke."

I didn't know how to break the news to her that it wasn't, so I kept my mouth shut . . . tight.

I spent the rest of the afternoon rewriting that list, with Ms. Adolf breathing down my neck every second. When we were done, our new list included fun-filled, action-packed activities like these:

1. Describe your favorite subject in school. *(Boring!)*
2. Share three facts about your country. *(Beyond boring!)*
3. Recite a poem in your native language. *(Give me a break!)*
4. Draw a picture of your flag. *(You've got to be kidding!)*
5. Do a native folk dance together. *(Not in this lifetime!)*

Even though I had never met Yoshi Morimoto, I knew he couldn't be that different from every ten-year-old I'd ever met, including me. I knew that if he ever saw that list, he would go running all the way back to Japan, even if it is an island country surrounded by water.

CHAPTER 5

I WAITED UNTIL AFTER DINNER to ask my parents if Yoshi could stay with us. I thought it would probably be okay with them, but you can never be totally sure when it comes to parents. There's always the possibility that they'll come up with some weird reason to say no—like you have to take a tango lesson with your mom, or baby-sit your sister's iguana. Don't laugh. I had to miss two sleepovers at Frankie's for just those reasons.

The minute we finished our beet soufflé and scrambled tofu with chestnuts, I jumped right up to clear the table. My rule is you can never be too helpful when you're about to ask your parents for something important.

"Wow," my sister, Emily, said as I stacked the dishes all the way up my arm. "Look who's clearing the table without even checking to see if it's his turn."

"Just trying to lend a hand. Isn't that what family is all about?" I said, flashing a big grin at my mom and dad.

"Sounds like somebody flunked another math test," Emily said. She's an excellent student and has never flunked anything in all her nine years. She doesn't have to. I do the flunking for both of us.

"Who wants a cup of tea?" I asked.

"Why, Hank, what a lovely idea," my mom said.

"Did you know they drink a lot of tea in Japan?" I asked, emphasizing the word *Japan*. Sometimes I surprise myself at how smooth I am. Did you like the way I just eased into the subject?

I went into the kitchen, set the dishes in the sink, and put some water in the teapot.

"What kind of tea does everybody want?" I called out, looking in the round blue tin where my mom keeps the tea bags. "We've got Almost Almond, Mostly Mint, or Relaxing Raspberry." There were three or four other kinds of tea bags in the tin, but I didn't offer them because their

27

names were too hard for me to read.

"Whatever sounds good, honey," my mom shouted through the swinging door. "Surprise us."

Naturally, I picked Relaxing Raspberry. I wanted my mom and dad to be nice and relaxed when I asked them about Yoshi. How could I face Ms. Adolf if my parents said no? It would be totally embarrassing.

When the tea was ready, I picked up the teapot and cups and pushed the swinging door to the dining room open with my butt. Suddenly, Katherine darted out from under the table. She ran right in front of me, her long tail swishing back and forth under my feet. I could feel myself starting to wobble badly. Luckily, I was able to spit out one word before my legs went completely out from under me:

"Teapot!" I shrieked.

My dad jumped up and grabbed the teapot from my hands. My mom snatched the cups just in time. As for me, I went flying over the iguana's tail and landed on the carpet. I lay there, flat on my stomach, facing eye to eye with the scaly beast. Katherine just flipped her gray-green tongue out and tapped me on the nose with it.

Emily couldn't stop laughing. Then she noticed that I was NOT laughing. She got real serious real fast.

"Hank, don't you dare yell at Kathy," she warned. "You know how upset she gets when she thinks you're mad at her."

Excuse me? The iguana gets upset? I was the one who just came in for an emergency tummy landing and got licked with her sandpapery tongue!

Ordinarily, I would have blasted Emily about her creepy, ugly, scaly, yucky lizard getting under my feet. But I was about to bring up an important subject with the parents, and this was not the time to pick a fight. So instead, I counted to five under my breath, then reached over and patted Katherine on the snout—even though what I really wanted to do was pound her into the rug.

"Accidents happen, old girl," I said. "I hope I didn't hurt your cute crusty tail."

Emily's jaw fell open so wide that I thought I was going to have to get a tow truck to haul it back up to her face.

"Wow, Hank. You were so sensitive to

Kathy's feelings," she said.

"Hey, if a big brother can't be nice to his sister's iguana, then what's the point of . . ."

I had no idea how to finish that sentence. I glanced at my parents out of the corner of my eye. My mom was smiling. She loves it when we get along. Even my dad looked up from his crossword puzzle for a second and gave me a little nod. Well, maybe little is too big to describe the nod. It was more of a slight eye twitch.

"Here, Dad, let me pour you a cup of tea," I said, jumping up.

I poured some of the hot tea into his cup. Then I put my hands together in front of me, turned to him, and bowed. I poured my mom a cup of tea and bowed at her, too.

"What's with all the bowing?" Emily said. "Did you do a silent but deadly, or something?"

"For your information, I am performing the Japanese tea ceremony," I told her.

"Well, for your information, we happen to live in New York," Emily said. "Not Japan."

"I thought it would be nice to practice for when Yoshi gets here," I said.

"Yoshi who?" my dad asked, barely looking up from his crossword puzzle.

"Yoshi Morimoto."

"Isn't that the Japanese chef on the cooking channel?" he asked. "Why would he want to stay here?"

"He doesn't."

"But you just said he did."

When my dad is in the middle of doing a crossword puzzle, he only listens with one ear, which means he only gets half of the conversation right.

"Dad, listen," I said. "Cancel the whole Japanese chef thought. Yoshi Morimoto is a fourth-grade kid who's coming to our school for Multi-Cultural Day. We, all of us, have been picked as his host family. He's going to stay here for two nights later this week if it's okay with you guys. And I just can't imagine that you would turn down the educational experience of the century."

"It's a lovely idea, honey," my mom said, "but I'm worried about the bathroom."

"What's wrong with the bathroom?" I asked.

"It needs new wallpaper, Hank. We can't

have a visitor from another country experience our peeling wallpaper."

See what I mean about parents? You think you know them, then at the last minute they come up with something weird and throw you a total curveball.

"Mom, the wallpaper is fine. We don't have to change anything in our apartment. The whole point is for Yoshi to see how a typical American family lives. He'll love it here."

"What do you think, Stan?" my mom asked my dad.

"I could show the boy my collection of mechanical pencils," my dad said. "I've got some pretty unique ones, you know."

"Great idea, Dad," I said. "I'll bet he's never seen that many mechanicals in one place before."

My dad nodded. He's very proud of his mechanical pencils, which he calls his m.p.'s. He has a whole desk drawer full of them in every color and every metal known to mankind.

"You have to ask your sister how she feels about having a visitor, Hank," my mom said. "It's her house, too."

"I think it sounds like fun," Emily said. "What do you think, Katherine?"

"Wait a minute," I complained. "Since when does the lizard get a vote?"

"She's a member of this family," said Emily. "But it's okay, because she votes yes. Don't you, Kathy?"

Emily took hold of one of Katherine's paws and raised it up in the air like she was voting. Katherine hissed. I guess iguanas aren't big fans of democracy.

Just then, our dog, Cheerio, who was asleep on the couch in the living room, woke up and ran over to our fireplace. He started to bark at the bricks, which is one of his hobbies when he's not licking the bricks or chasing his tail.

"I think Cheerio wants to vote, too," Emily said.

"Hey, boy," I said as I sat down next to him. "How do you vote? Say yip if it's yes."

Cheerio rolled over on his back, and I scratched him on this little white spot under his chin where he loves to be scratched. He yipped, softly, but it was a definite yip.

"Then it's unanimous," my mom said. "The

whole family votes yes to have Yoshi stay here."

I ran to my backpack and got the permission slip. My dad signed it with his red metallic mechanical pencil, and then we all hugged.

Yoshi was coming to our house. It was a done deal. And done in Zipzer style, too. That meant two parents, two kids, one hissing iguana, and one dachshund barking at the fireplace bricks. Just your typical American family.

CHAPTER 6

THE NEXT DAY WAS TUESDAY, and our class spent the day preparing for Yoshi and his dad to arrive. They were coming on Wednesday morning and staying until Friday. Yoshi was going to spend Wednesday in our class and then sleep over at my house. The next day, Thursday, was the big Multi-Cultural Day celebration for the whole school. Yoshi and his dad, Mr. Morimoto, were the guests of honor. Everyone in my grade was assigned to bring in a dish from another country. We were going to put all the dishes out for a huge buffet lunch in the Multi-Purpose Room and have a celebration meal.

In the morning, Ms. Adolf made us clean out our desks for Yoshi's arrival. Personally, I don't see why we had to. It's not like they don't have messy desks in Japan.

When I asked her why we had to clean our

desks, Ms. Adolf said, "We are putting our best foot forward, Henry."

I think if we're putting our best foot forward, then she should take off those icky gray shoes she wears every day and put on some cool green and yellow Nikes—or at least spray the insides with odor eaters.

Ms. Adolf walked up and down the aisles with her roll book and put a check next to your name when she thought your desk was clean enough. I was the last one to get a check. I filled up one whole wastebasket with the stuff she made me throw away. There was some really good stuff in my desk, too. A half-eaten granola bar that I was saving in case of emergency. Hey, you never know when hunger will strike. A dried-up blueberry-scented marker that still smelled a tiny bit like blueberries. I was going to miss that marker. Oh, and the seven paper clips bent into triangles that I use to play desk hockey.

After lunch, Principal Love came to our class to give us a lecture on how we were supposed to behave around Yoshi. Principal Love is a short bald man, but his voice sounds like he should be an NBA player with bushy black hair.

"Each of you is representing not only this school, but this city, this state—all of America!" Principal Love said in his tall man, bushy hair voice. "You are representing us when you walk, when you talk, when you skip, and when you hop. You are representing us when you raise your hand, but not when you don't raise your hand."

Oh, in case this isn't making any sense to you, don't worry. I forgot to tell you that no one ever understands what Principal Love is saying. I'm pretty sure he doesn't either, because there is always a look of confusion in his eyes when he lectures us.

I knew I couldn't look at Frankie or we'd start to laugh. I did glance over at Ashley. She looked like she was hypnotized, just staring at the mole on Principal Love's cheek. Oh, I forgot to tell you about that, too. Principal Love has this mole on his face that's shaped like the Statue of Liberty without the torch. When he talks, it looks like the Statue of Liberty is doing the hula.

As Principal Love droned on, Ashley looked over at me and rolled her eyes back until you could only see the white parts. That's not easy to do, but Ashley can do lots of body tricks like that. I knew I couldn't laugh, but I couldn't hold it in. A little snorting sound leaked out through my nose. Ms. Adolf shot me the death look. I held my nose and pushed that snort all the way back into my brain.

During art period, a bunch of us volunteered to go to Mr. Rock's room in the basement to make a welcome sign for Yoshi. His room is the biggest one in our school, so we had plenty of room to spread out and make a really big sign. Mr. Rock is the music teacher at PS 87 and a really cool guy. In fact, he's the one who first suggested that I be tested for learning differences. He has learning differences, too, but he always points out that they didn't stop him from achieving his dream of teaching.

Mr. Rock rolled out a long sheet of brown paper while Frankie and Hector Ruiz mixed up paints. Ryan Shimozato had brought a slip of paper with the words WELCOME, YOSHI written in Japanese characters. Ryan's dad, who was born in Japan, wrote it out for him. We were going to try to copy it onto the sign.

Those characters looked really complicated. Ryan said there are almost two thousand of them that combine to make up the Japanese language. Boy, it's a good thing I wasn't born in Japan. If I had to learn to write all those characters, I never would have gotten out of kindergarten.

"Mr. Rock, can I decorate the sign with rhinestones?" Ashley asked. "I brought some pink ones from home. Maybe they'll remind Yoshi of the cherry blossoms in springtime in Japan."

A blast of dragon breath came shooting in from the hallway door. I knew that breath. It was Nick McKelty breath—the breath of peanut butter turned bad. I spun around and, sure enough, the big jerk was slithering into Mr. Rock's room. Who asked him to help?

"Rhinestones!" laughed Nick McKelty. "How girlie is that!"

"Ashley is expressing her creativity," Mr. Rock said to him. "Everyone in here is free to be creative."

"Ha, ha, ha," Ashley whispered to McKelty as she whipped out a baggie of rhinestones and her glue stick. "I ought to rhinestone your mouth shut."

Frankie and Hector finished mixing the paints, and brought them over to the paper. Ryan and I were ready to start outlining the Japanese letters. McKelty reached over, stuck his beefy arm in front of everyone, and grabbed a paintbrush, almost knocking the jelly jars of paint over.

"I'm one of the best artists on the Upper West Side," he said, like anyone believed him. "I won an art trophy once, and it's so big, I can hardly fit it in my room."

We call that the McKelty Factor: truth times one hundred. No one even pays attention when he brags like that. But since no one has ever been to his house for a play date—except Luke Whitman once—we couldn't really catch him in the lie this time.

"Oh, by the way, dude, we're painting in Japanese," Frankie said to him. "You know how to do that, don't you?"

McKelty squinted down at the Japanese letters on Ryan's paper. When he looked up, his big face was even blanker than usual. He didn't have a clue what to do. His eyes scanned the room for someone to pick on.

"Hey, Zipperhead," McKelty shouted over to me. "This is a good job for you. Your hand-writing looks like Japanese even when you're writing in English."

"That's enough of that kind of talk," Mr. Rock said to McKelty. "We don't make fun of anyone in this room."

I told you Mr. Rock was cool.

"I'm just saying what's true," McKelty said with a shrug of his beefy shoulders. "Zipper Boy's writing looks like he does it with his big toe."

Mr. Rock walked over to Nick and took the paintbrush out of his hand.

"The door is this way," he said, pointing to the hall.

"Huh?" said Nick. "I know where the door is."

"Then use it and leave," said Mr. Rock. "When you can stop making fun of other people, you're welcome back."

McKelty turned all red in the face. He just stood there, but so did Mr. Rock. Finally, Nick the Tick muttered something under his disgusting breath and stomped out.

41

I wanted to jump up and down and shout. Man, was it ever good to see McKelty sent out of the room.

Mr. Rock came over to me and handed me a paintbrush.

"Now, Hank, I believe you've got some painting to do," he said, giving me a pretty firm shoulder squeeze.

I took the brush and started to paint. I decided then and there that as soon as I got the chance, the first person I was going to introduce Yoshi to was Mr. Rock.

He's what I call putting your best foot forward for America.

CHAPTER 7

I WAS SO EXCITED ABOUT MEETING YOSHI that I couldn't sleep all night. By the time the school bell rang the next morning, I was already glued to the window of my classroom, staring out at 78th Street. Every time a car pulled up in front of my school, I was sure Yoshi and his dad would step out of it. I couldn't wait for them to get there.

I don't know if you've already got a picture in your mind of what Yoshi would look like, but I sure did.

In my mind, he would be smallish, probably about my height. (Some people might call that short, but I like the word *smallish* better.) Of course, he'd have jet-black hair that would probably be cut in floppy bangs straight across his forehead. I had seen that hairdo in all the pictures in the books Ms. Adolf had brought us on Japan. I thought he'd probably be wearing a uniform. Ms. Adolf told us that most Japanese kids wear uniforms to school. He'd be walking quietly and respectfully next to his father because Japanese children are taught to be very well-behaved around older people. But I'm here to tell you that Yoshi Morimoto was nothing like what I expected. Not even a little bit.

When I first caught sight of him rounding the corner from Amsterdam Avenue onto 78th Street, Yoshi was whizzing along the sidewalk on a black skateboard with bright orange flames. He had some pretty cool moves, too, shooting ahead of his dad and then doing a 360 to give his dad time to catch up. He was taller than me, maybe even taller than Frankie. And that was no uniform he was wearing. He was dressed in denim jeans and a New York T-shirt with a Big Apple on it, the kind you can buy in Times Square. He had on silver sneakers that looked like they had just been flown in on a spaceship from another galaxy. They might have been the coolest shoes I've ever seen.

And forget the floppy bang thing I talked

about before. His hair was gelled into a porcupine. A really good-looking porcupine.

"Here he is!" I shouted.

Everyone in the class rushed over to the window. Katie Sperling was the first to get there. She pressed her face against the glass and looked out.

"Wow," she sighed. "He's hot."

"Yeah," Frankie said. "He's cool."

"That's an awesome skateboard," Hector Ruiz said.

"I wonder if I could get my hair to do that," said Luke.

"Ms. Adolf, can we go downstairs and say hi to Yoshi?" I asked.

"I don't think that's necessary, Henry," she said. "Principal Love is there to welcome him and escort him up here."

"But Principal Love is the most boring person on Earth," I answered.

Hank Zipzer, did you just say that?

I slapped my hand over my mouth. What was I thinking? You can't just insult your principal in front of your teacher. But the words fell out of my mouth before I could stop myself.

Everyone in the class was laughing hysterically. I closed my eyes and waited for Ms. Adolf to get really mad.

"You have a point," Ms. Adolf said. "He is a tad on the long-winded side. Actually, *boring* is a good word."

Wow! Maybe there is a human being underneath all those gray clothes.

Ms. Adolf let us go downstairs to greet Yoshi, all thirty-two of us.

"That was an awesome thing to say," Frankie said to me as we hurried down the stairwell. "My man Zip, telling it like it is."

My big mouth is always getting me in trouble. For once, it had done something right.

CHAPTER 8

WHEN WE GOT DOWNSTAIRS, Principal Love was standing on the steps by the school entrance, making his welcome-to-our-school speech. I'm no fashion expert, but even I could tell he had some pretty weird clothes on. Principal Love usually wears these nerdy black Velcro shoes that squeak when he walks down the linoleum halls. Those are bad enough. But on special days, he wears another pair of sneakers that he's painted in our school colors, blue and yellow. I'm not kidding. One shoe is blue, and the other is yellow. He had hauled out those beauties especially for Mr. Morimoto and Yoshi's arrival.

As if wearing the blue and yellow shoes wasn't goofy enough, Principal Love also was wearing a fluffy blue and yellow scarf that his wife knit for him. It had long, hairy tassels on the ends that reached down almost to his knees. He looked more like a crazed clown than a principal, especially compared with Mr. Morimoto. He, on the other hand, was wearing a black overcoat and black leather gloves, and his hair was all slicked back and classy.

I kept watching Yoshi as Principal Love yapped on and on like he was the president of New York City. Yoshi was looking down toward Amsterdam Avenue, checking out the cart on the corner that sells hot dogs and warm pretzels. I was thinking that maybe I'd ask him later if he wanted to stop by there for a hot dog. Then, a sudden thought struck me:

This kid probably doesn't speak English!

I mean, why would he? He lives in Tokyo.

Wow. This was going to be a problem. The only words I could say in Japanese were *ee-chee* and *nee*. Unless Yoshi was really into counting, we weren't going to have much to talk about.

Wait a minute, Hankster. You've got hands. People talk with their hands all the time.

I thought I'd give it a try. Yoshi was still watching the guy at the hot dog cart who was grilling up a new batch of hot sausages with onions. I coughed really loud to get Yoshi's attention, then tried to make eye contact with him. Finally, he looked over at me. I flashed him a sign with my hands that I thought said, *"Hey, buddy, let's swing by that hot dog cart later and chow down."*

Yoshi looked a little confused, so I flashed him the sign again. I thought my sign language was pretty clear. I pointed to the cart, then pantomimed squirting mustard on a foot-long hot dog and eating it. I was rubbing my stomach to signal how yummy the hot dog was when, suddenly, I felt Frankie tapping me on the shoulder.

"Where are you, Zip? He's talking to you," he whispered.

I looked up and realized that Principal Love had stopped his speech and was speaking to me.

"Do you need to be excused, Mr. Zipzer?" he was saying.

"Who me?"

"I thought perhaps from the way you were moving, that you need to—you know—use the boys' facilities."

Facilities? What was he talking about? The

science lab? The supply closet?

"The restroom," Principal Love said, talking out of the side of his mouth as if no one else would hear him.

Oh! He thought I had to go to the bathroom! No wonder. I realized that my hand was on my stomach, and I was rubbing it in big circles.

Everyone was laughing. I wished I had a huge bottle of invisible ink so I could pour it all over myself and disappear.

"I'm fine, Principal Love. Really I am. Go on. I'm very interested in what you have to say. We all are. Aren't we, guys?"

There was a lot of snorting from the other kids as everyone choked back a laugh. Principal Love went on with his speech. Ms. Adolf flashed me an icy look.

"Can you please try to act normal for once?" Frankie whispered to me. "She's watching you. If you keep on screwing up, she's not going to allow Yoshi to stay at your house."

"And if he doesn't stay over, I'll die," Ashley whispered.

"What's it to you?" I asked her.

"What's it to me?" she repeated. "Look at

him. He's soooo cute."

What was going on here? Ashley Wong, my best friend and pal, talking like an airhead?

It turns out that Ashley wasn't the only kid in class who was in love with Yoshi. Everyone, boy or girl, immediately thought he was the coolest person they had ever seen. He just had that look about him, the kind of look that says, *"I'm me, and there are not many others like me around."*

When Principal Love finished his welcoming speech, which seemed like it lasted a thousand hours, everyone in my class immediately surrounded Yoshi. Ms. Adolf clapped three times to try to get our attention.

"Let's take Yoshi to our classroom, pupils," she said. "You'll have plenty of time to get to know him there."

Ms. Adolf started up the stairs and we all followed her, herding Yoshi into the middle of our group. Hector Ruiz carried his skateboard. Ryan Shimozato walked next to him.

"Sensei," Ryan said, pointing to Ms. Adolf.

Yoshi smiled and nodded.

"Sensei," he repeated.

"That means 'teacher' in Japanese," Ryan

explained to a bunch of us who were crowding around.

"It's so great that you learned Japanese from your dad," Ashley said.

"Actually, I learned it from *The Karate Kid*," Ryan answered. "That's what they call the karate teacher, Mr. Miyagi."

"I love that movie," Thomas McAndrews said. "I've seen it a million times. We've got all three on DVD."

"Oh, yeah? Well, we've got ten DVDs of it," piped up Nick McKelty. "Maybe even twelve."

"Right, McKelty. And my name's Bernice," Frankie said.

We all laughed.

"*Karate Kid* is a cool movie," someone said as we trudged upstairs.

I looked around to see who was talking. I didn't recognize the voice. I thought maybe it was Luke Whitman doing one of his bad movie star impressions that all sound alike.

"Mr. Miyagi kicks butt," said the same voice.

I looked around again, and this time I saw who was talking.

It was Yoshi!

CHAPTER 9

WHO WOULD HAVE GUESSED Yoshi could speak Japanese *and* English? That's two entire languages, which is pretty amazing when you think about it. I mean, I have enough trouble just with English, and I've been trying to speak it since I was born. The idea of me learning another whole language is . . . well . . . it's not even an idea.

Yoshi's English wasn't totally perfect, but he could say a lot. He told us that at his school in Tokyo, which is called the Bancho School, kids are taught English starting in kindergarten. He and some of his friends also learn English with a special tutor after school. That's like what I do with Dr. Berger, who gives me special tutoring in reading comprehension after school. I guess it's not exactly the same. I mean, those guys have an excuse for needing a tutor in English.

They're Japanese. What's my excuse?

It turns out that Yoshi is also a total fan of American movies and TV, and watching them helped him learn English, too. After we got to class, Luke Whitman wouldn't settle down. He kept doing his zombie walk where he crashes into everybody's desk like he's a dead guy. It was funny at first, but then, when he wouldn't stop, it got annoying. Finally, Yoshi looked at Luke and said, "Oh, behave!" just like Austin Powers says in the movies. We all laughed so much, Ms. Adolf had to clap her hands about thirty times to get *us* to behave.

Ms. Adolf kicked off Yoshi's day in our class with fun, fun, fun like only she can come up with. She must have gone to the College for Teachers Who Know How to Ruin Fun for Everyone. I'll bet she was the best student they ever had, too.

For starters, she had us all draw a picture of the Japanese flag. Fortunately, it's a plain white flag with nothing but a solid red circle in the middle, so we were done with our drawings in about thirty seconds. She made us give them all to Yoshi. The poor guy was sitting there at a desk, with thirty-three red circles stacked up in front of him. He didn't really know what to say. I mean, what do you say to that? *Wow, they really are so round.* Or, *Where's the closest wastebasket?*

He was very polite, though, you could tell. He flipped through the red circles and acted like he was really impressed.

"Cowabunga!" he said, sounding a whole lot like Bart Simpson.

"Hey, Yosh Man, you watch *The Simpsons?*" Frankie asked.

"I'm sure he doesn't," Ms. Adolf answered. "That youngster Bartholomew Simpson sets such a rude example for children."

The last thing you want to do is get into a conversation with Ms. Adolf about any TV show, let alone *The Simpsons.* Once, she told us that she doesn't think children should ever watch cartoons, because they're silly. She believes there's no point in being silly when you can be serious about history or alphabetizing.

"Bart Simpson kicks butt," Yoshi whispered to Frankie and me, when Ms. Adolf was erasing the board. I stuck up my hand and he high-fived it.

This kid Yoshi Morimoto was okay. He was

more than okay. He was awesome.

Heather Payne raised her hand and asked if she could share something she had brought in. Ms. Adolf, who loves Heather Payne more than life itself because Heather always does everything right, smiled at her and said of course she could. If I had asked to share something, she would have smiled and said a big, fat no.

Heather reached into a brown paper supermarket bag she had brought from home and pulled out a black and red flowered dress. Well, it wasn't exactly a dress, but it was a dress-coat kind of thing. Heather walked to the front of the class and put it on.

"Does anyone know what this is?" she asked, turning around a couple of times like a model.

"Dracula's bathrobe?" Nick McKelty shouted out. Then he opened up his gigantic mouth and laughed like he had just told the funniest joke ever invented. You could see bits of his breakfast burrito still wedged in between his two front teeth. No one else in the class even chuckled, and Yoshi looked at him like the moron that he was. I thought Heather Payne was going to cry.

"That's not funny, Nick," she said, which was

the first thing Heather Payne ever said that I completely agreed with. Well, that's not exactly true. Once she said that she was allergic to shrimp, and I am, too.

"I know what it is," Katie Sperling said, before Ms. Adolf could even call on her. "It's a kimona." She turned to Yoshi and gave him the most beautiful smile you have ever seen. "Isn't that right, Yoshi?"

If Katie Sperling ever smiled at me like that, I would melt into a little puddle of cherry Jell-O right in front of her eyes. But Yoshi actually got embarrassed. He looked down at his feet and shifted around in his chair.

"Kimono," he said. "There's an *o* at the end."

"Oh! Thank you, Yoshi," Katie said, batting her green eyes at him.

"The kimono is what traditional Japanese women wear," Heather said. "My neighbor Mrs. Yamazaki let me bring this one in to show you."

Heather walked up and down the aisles so we could all see the kimono. Suddenly, the door opened and Principal Love came in with Mr.

Morimoto right next to him. They were on a tour of the school. Mr. Morimoto smiled at Heather.

"You look lovely in your kimono," he said, bowing to her. "My wife, Yoshi's mother, was married in a white kimono with cherry blossoms on it, which is worn in the springtime."

Ashley's hand shot up in the air.

"Did it have any pink rhinestones on it?" she asked.

Mr. Morimoto smiled. "No, it did not," he said. "But that sounds like a very beautiful idea."

"Speaking of beautiful ideas, I saw a package of Mallomars in the teachers' lounge this morning," Principal Love said to Mr. Morimoto. "How about if we head over there for a mid-morning snack? Like I always say, the Mallomar is the classic American cookie. Yes sir, the Mallomar is the classic American cookie."

Principal Love always says everything twice. We're used to it, and we just stop listening after the first time he says something—sometimes even before.

"There are so many ways to eat a

Mallomar," Principal Love went on, raising his voice so we all could hear, as if we wanted to. "Personally, I like to peel off the chocolate first, and then suck the marshmallow into my mouth, flattening it with my tongue until it's nice and gooey. I save the cookie part to be dunked into cold milk."

His Statue of Liberty mole was doing jumping jacks now, which it does when he gets excited about his topic. Poor Mr. Morimoto. He had no idea what Principal Love was talking about.

"My brother Lester starts with the cookie part and saves the chocolate-covered marshmallow for last," Principal Love said. "There's more than one way to skin a Mallomar, that's what I always say. There's more than one way to skin a Mallomar."

Principal Love threw his head back and laughed really loud. Mr. Morimoto smiled politely, but I'll bet he was looking for an emergency exit. If I were him, I would have been.

"I'll see you tomorrow, Yoshi," he said. "It is your honor to spend the night with one of your fellow students."

"Oh, no, sir. The honor is mine," I said. "I

am the fellow student."

I couldn't help it. It just shot out of my mouth, and then I smiled from ear to ear. I looked over at Yoshi.

"We'll have fun at my house," I said to him.

"*Ikeru,*" he said to me.

"What's that mean?" I asked.

"That's what we say in Japan. It means 'that's cool,' " he said.

"*Ikeru,* dude," I said. "Right back at you."

He held up his hand and I high-fived it.

Mr. Morimoto smiled at Yoshi and bowed to me. He turned to leave the room, but old Principal Love was right behind him. I could hear him starting in on why Mallomars were better than Fig Newtons as his Velcro shoes squeaked out the door and chased Mr. Morimoto down the hallway.

CHAPTER 1

Having Yoshi in our class was the most fun I've had in school all year.

When we went to the art room, our teacher Ms. Anderson said we were supposed to be drawing a still life of vegetables. Instead, she let Yoshi show us how to draw a really neat superhero from a Japanese comic book. He was a very good artist. As he outlined the character, his tongue curled back and forth along his lower lip. You could tell he was concentrating really hard.

At recess, we played softball. Frankie pitched and Yoshi hit a homerun over the Amsterdam Avenue fence. He said he wants to be a professional baseball player when he grows up. Unfortunately, he likes those stinking Yankees, just like Frankie. I'm a Mets fan myself because they are truly the best team in the U. S. of A.

In music, Mr. Rock had brought in some tapes of traditional Japanese string music, and we listened to them. I won't lie to you. I thought they were a little on the screechy side, but Frankie liked them. He said they sounded like the music his mom plays when she's teaching yoga class. Then Yoshi reached into his backpack and pulled out a CD he had brought with him of a new Japanese rap group. We put that on, and Mr. Rock even did a little break dancing. I couldn't understand the words, of course. But the music sounded like the stuff we listen to here.

At lunch, Yoshi took out some chopsticks he had brought with him and tried to teach us how to use them. Most everyone was terrible at it. It was Swedish meatball day, and let me tell you, there were lots of Swedish meatballs rolling around our cafeteria floor. Ashley's grandmother had taught her how to use chopsticks, so she was great at it. She and Yoshi had a chopstick battle to see who could pick up the smallest bit of food without dropping it. When Ashley won, Yoshi bowed to her and she got the giggles. I don't think I've ever seen Ashley get the giggles like that.

I was a little worried about our sleepover that night. After all the fun things we had done that day, I wondered how I would come up with anything really interesting to do. Suddenly, hanging out and watching TV seemed kind of dull.

In the afternoon, Frankie came up with one of his usual brilliant ideas. He made up a game show called "Ask the Yosh Man," and somehow, he talked Ms. Adolf into letting us play it. When Frankie Townsend flashes you the Big Dimple and turns on the charm, even teachers can't say no.

Here's how we played: Frankie put Yoshi in a chair in front of the class. Then each person got to ask him one question. Yoshi could either tell the truth, or make up a fake answer. Then we'd get to yell TRUE if we thought it was the true answer, or FALSE if we thought he was making it up.

"What's your favorite sport?" Thomas McAndrews asked him first.

"Baseball," Yoshi said.

"TRUE," we all shouted.

"Do you have brothers and sisters?" Kim Paulson asked.

"I have one sister named Bernice," Yoshi said, grinning at Frankie.

"FALSE," we shouted.

"Have you ever eaten a raw snail?" Luke Whitman asked.

"No, but I eat raw octopus," answered Yoshi.

"FALSE," we shouted. But we were wrong on that one. Yoshi told us people in Japan eat raw octopus often. Luke Whitman said if he ate octopus, he'd spit out the suction cups on the tentacles.

"Have you ever seen a real live sumo wrestler?" asked Ashley.

"Yes, my uncle is one," Yoshi said.

"TRUE," we all shouted. And it was! How cool is it to have an uncle who's a sumo wrestler? I thought it was great that my uncle Gary owns a video store and gives us discounts on DVDs. But Yoshi had an uncle who weighed 432 pounds and wore a diaper.

"What's your favorite food?" Ashley asked.

"Enchiladas," Yoshi answered.

"FALSE," we all shouted, laughing.

Guess what? We were wrong on that one!

Imagine our surprise when Yoshi said his absolute most favorite food was cheese enchiladas. He had only had them once when their school had a visitor from Mexico, but he had never forgotten them.

A lightbulb went off in my head. Suddenly, I knew what we were going to do that night. We were going to make a dish for the buffet lunch tomorrow. Chef Hank was going to teach Yoshi Morimoto how to make cheese enchiladas.

You're probably wondering if I'd ever made cheese enchiladas before.

You know what? There's a first time for everything!

CHAPTER 11

AFTER SCHOOL, we were all going to walk back to our apartment building together—Frankie, Emily, Yoshi, and me, with Robert tagging not far behind. Ashley had to go to soccer practice, so she was going to meet up with us later, after dinner.

While we waited on the front steps of school for my parents to pick us up, Yoshi showed us a few of his skateboard moves. He was working on perfecting his kick-flip and he actually did one—not once, but twice!

Emily kept staring at him with that same goo-goo-eyed expression that Ashley had when she first saw him. On a scale of one to ten, I'd say Emily was interested in Yoshi one thousand and fifty-seven.

"There she goes again," Frankie whispered to me as he watched Emily staring at Yoshi.

"She's doing that eye thing she does at Robert."

"The girl is a goo-goo-eye machine," I whispered back. "It's so embarrassing."

Robert kept trying to get Emily to notice him. He was jealous of how much attention she was paying to Yoshi, no doubt about it. Emily and Robert have a special nerd-to-nerd kind of connection. Let's just say they've bonded over their love of the wonderful world of reptiles. So every time Yoshi would attempt a kick-flip, Robert would turn to Emily and say something like, "Snakes have no eyelids or ear holes."

Poor little guy. No one cared—not even Emily, at that moment.

I was expecting to see my mom and dad, so I was really surprised when Papa Pete came jogging up 78th Street to our school. He waved to Mr. Baker, the crossing guard, and panted to a stop right in front of us. He was breathing pretty hard, although he's in good shape for an almost sixty-eight-year-old grandpa.

As soon as Yoshi saw Papa Pete approach us, he hopped off his skateboard, came over to him, and bowed. That was a strange sight. My grandpa looks like a big, warm, fuzzy grizzly bear in a strawberry-red jogging suit. He's definitely not the kind of person you bow to.

"Hello, grandkids," Papa Pete said, reaching out to give each of us a pinch on the cheek. I was curious to see if he was going to pinch Yoshi, too, but he didn't. Instead, he bowed back.

"You must be Yoshi," he said. "I'm Papa Pete, Hank's grandfather."

Yoshi bowed again. "It is an honor to meet you, *ojiisan*."

"Hey, Yosh, you can call him Papa Pete," Frankie said. "We all do."

"In Japan, we call older men *ojiisan*," Yoshi said. "Out of respect."

Papa Pete broke out into a big smile and twirled the end of his long handlebar mustache with his fingers.

"Right! It's about time I got a little respect around here," he said, giving Frankie and me a playful chuck under the chin. Then he turned to Yoshi. "How would you like to come with *ojiisan* on a little 'Welcome to America' celebration?" he said. "I have in mind some bowling and a root-beer float."

68

"I have never seen root beer float," said Yoshi. "I didn't know it could."

We all had a really good laugh, including Papa Pete.

"We're going to have a good time, Yoshi, my boy," he said.

And then he did just what I knew he was going to do. He reached out and gave Yoshi a big pinch on the cheek. Yoshi seemed surprised, but I think he liked it. There isn't anybody who doesn't like Papa Pete. He is the greatest, warmest, funniest, smartest grandpa around.

We headed down Amsterdam Avenue toward McKelty's Roll 'N Bowl, which is Papa Pete's home away from home. He's a champion bowler, and a champion root-beer-float drinker, too. By the way, in case you recognize the McKelty name, the bowling alley is owned by Nick the Tick's father. He's a nice man. No one can understand how that idiot he has for a son got born into his family.

"Where's Mom and Dad?" I asked Papa Pete as we dodged our way along the crowded sidewalk. "I thought they were coming to pick us up."

"They're still at the apartment," Papa Pete answered. "They're busy."

"Doing what?"

"Your mother got it into her head that they had to put up new wallpaper in the bathroom," he answered. "I don't know why she picked today of all days to do it."

I knew, but I didn't say anything.

"She thought they'd be finished by now," Papa Pete went on. "But—" He lowered his voice to a whisper. "There was a little accident involving the iguana and a can of wallpaper paste."

Emily, who has all-powerful hearing when you even breathe anything about Katherine, flew into a total panic.

"What happened to Katherine?" she asked. "Is she hurt?"

"Katherine is fine," Papa Pete reassured her. "She stepped in the wallpaper paste and got stuck to the kitchen floor for a few minutes, that's all."

"You mean she was glued to the linoleum?" Emily yelled.

"We soaked her feet in water and got her

unstuck," Papa Pete explained. "She's absolutely as good as new. Except she keeps smelling her toes."

Frankie and I burst out laughing.

"Oh, so you think it's funny that Kathy was stuck to the floor!" Emily shouted at me.

"No, Emily." I could barely answer because I was holding my sides, I was laughing so hard. "I don't *think* it's funny, I *know* it's funny."

"Hank, when will you grow up?" she said.

"In about another eight years," I howled.

I was behaving badly and I knew it. But I couldn't stop. Yoshi was behaving much better than I was. He reached out and patted Emily's arm.

"I would like to meet your lizard," he said to her in a kind voice.

"You would?" she said. "Oh, Kathy would love that."

Emily smiled so big, you could almost see her molars. And she had another goo-goo-eye attack, too. Boy, that really got to Robert.

"Actually, Yoshi," he said, "I don't recommend that. The iguana can be very moody around new people. I don't think Kathy would like you."

Wow. Robert Upchurch gets grumpy. I guess love will do that to a guy.

"Robert! Of course Kathy wants to meet Yoshi," Emily said.

"How do you know?" I asked. "Did she tell you?"

"As a matter of fact, she did," Emily said. "We have a special way of communicating. I know what she's thinking, and she knows what I'm thinking."

"Actually, I have developed the knack of iguana communication myself," Robert said. He had that annoying little bubble thing going on in his throat, and he needed to clear it real bad. Poor guy. I didn't have the heart to tell him.

It didn't matter, anyway. We had arrived at McKelty's Roll 'N Bowl and we were already running up the stairs to get our bowling shoes on.

It probably won't surprise you to learn that Yoshi was a very good bowler. And you should have seen him on the arcade games. Was there anything this kid couldn't do? He had magic fingers and killer concentration. I hardly ever play arcade games because my mind always wanders and I'm never able to win.

After we bowled, Papa Pete treated us all to root-beer floats. Yoshi thought the float was the most delicious thing he'd ever tasted—next to enchiladas.

After we had slurped down the last speck of float, Papa Pete let us play one game of air hockey before we had to leave. Yoshi and I were neck and neck, and Frankie was watching, when guess who showed up. I'll give you a hint—rotten egg bordering on vomit breath.

You got it. Nick McKelty. He hangs out there a lot because it's his dad's place.

"I got winners," he said, hunkering down and leaning his rashy elbows on the table.

"Sorry, McKelty," I told him. "We have to go after this game."

"What's the big rush?"

"My grandpa's going to take us to Gristediano's."

"To the supermarket!" he snorted. "You Zipzers really know how to have a good time. What are you going to do after that? Introduce Yoshi to plastic bags at the dry cleaners? Or maybe get wild and go to Drago's Shoe Repair for some new heels?"

Why couldn't you ever just have a regular conversation with this guy? Why was he always on your case?

"For your info, dude," Frankie told him, "we are going to buy supplies to make enchiladas. We're bringing them for the Multi-Cultural Day Lunch tomorrow."

"Oh, yeah," McKelty said. "Wait until you see the pigs in a blanket that I'm bringing. They'll be a million times better."

"Pigs in a blanket?" Frankie said. "You mean those little hot dogs wrapped up in biscuit dough?"

"Not just regular hot dogs, Townsend," McKelty said. "These are special hot dogs. My dad got them from—"

McKelty stopped for a minute. You could just feel his slow brain trying to come up with some outrageous story we were all supposed to believe. Frankie didn't give him the chance.

"I know, dude," Frankie interrupted. "Your dad got them from the King of Hot Dog Land, who he met while sitting in the floor seats at the

Knicks game just before he slept over at the White House while teaching the president to bowl."

"How'd you know?" McKelty said.

We just laughed. Yoshi laughed, too. I'm sure he didn't actually understand all the words we were saying, but he got the picture about McKelty. A jerk is a jerk in any language.

"You're supposed to bring a dish from another country tomorrow," Robert said to McKelty. "That's why they call it the Multi-Cultural Day Lunch."

"So what's your point?" McKelty asked.

"The point is pigs in a blanket aren't from another country," I said.

"They are, too," said McKelty. "They're from Kansas."

"News flash, Big Dude. Kansas isn't a country," Frankie said.

"I knew that," McKelty growled. "I just wanted to see if you did."

"Right," Frankie said. "And my name is Bernice."

That cracks Yoshi up every time Frankie says it.

I glanced over at McKelty just to enjoy the look on his face. In that one second, Yoshi shot the puck past me and scored the winning goal.

"He shoots, he scores," he said, in absolutely perfect English.

"Where'd you learn that?" I asked him.

"PlayStation NHL hockey game," Yoshi answered with a shrug.

And they say video games aren't educational.

CHAPTER 12

PAPA PETE SAYS YOU SHOULD NEVER GO TO the grocery store without a list. While he was saying good-bye to his buddies at the bowling alley, we decided to take his advice. Frankie, Yoshi, and I sat down to make a list of what we needed to get at Gristediano's to make our enchiladas. Robert and Emily refused to participate. When you read the list, you'll see why.

OUR GROCERY STORE LIST
By Hank Zipzer, Frankie Townsend, and
Yoshi Morimoto

1. Get all the things you need to make enchiladas.
2. We wish we knew what those were, but we don't have a clue!
3. Well, that's not totally true. We know it's not broccoli or octopus.

4. Octopus and cheese enchiladas. Barf-o-rama!
5. Help!
6. We're stuck in this list and we can't get out!
7. How should I know what's in an enchilada? I'm from Japan!
8. Enchilada, schmintzalada! We'll figure it out later!

I know. You don't have to tell me. It's a stupid list. But hey, it was really funny at the time. I guess you had to be there.

Emily said we were acting like dumb boys. Robert said we were acting like immature boys. But I say this to you: We're only ten. We're entitled to lose it once in a while.

CHAPTER 13

THIS IS THE KIND OF GUY PAPA PETE IS. He took our list and looked it over. He didn't say one tiny word about how silly or stupid it was. All he said was, "Come on, kids. Let's get cracking. We got a batch of schmintzaladas to make."

Papa Pete is an expert cook. He started the Crunchy Pickle and ran it for his whole life until he retired and turned it over to my mom a couple of years ago. Almost everything in that deli is made from his recipes. Potato salad, red cabbage coleslaw, pastrami sandwiches with Russian dressing, tuna melts with tangy cheddar, black bean soup with sour cream. Everything tastes delicious. Except for the stuff my mom makes. She says she's trying to bring deli food into the twenty-first century, but I think she should have left it back in the twentieth century when Papa Pete was cooking.

Papa Pete told us he knew what was in enchiladas, and I trusted him completely. Anything he cooks comes out great.

We walked over to Gristediano's and cruised through the aisles, pushing our cart. Papa Pete called out the ingredients for the enchiladas, and we raced around the aisles to find them. We got tortillas and tomato sauce and cheese and garlic and a can of jalapeño peppers and sour cream. Then Papa Pete took us to the spice aisle.

"Now for a little zing!" he said, pointing to rows and rows of spice jars.

I looked through the spice jars. I saw curry and sage and dried parsley and cinnamon, but I didn't see anything called Zing.

Papa Pete ran his finger along the jars until he came to one that said Hot Chili Powder. It was filled with a dark red ground-up spice.

"This," he said, tossing the jar into our cart, "is what you need to give your enchiladas a little zing."

"I don't know what is zing," Yoshi said.

"Zing is what puts hair on your chest," Papa Pete told him.

"Eeuuuww, who wants that?" said Emily.

"It's an expression, my darling grand-daughter," Papa Pete said. "It refers to the kind of food that packs a wallop. Kicks up your taste buds. Puts a little spice in your life. Explodes on your tongue."

"Like wasabi," Yoshi said.

"Exactly," Papa Pete said, holding his finger up in the air like a nutty professor I saw in a movie once. "You've had wasabi, Hankie. Remember that spicy green horseradish you ate at Planet Sushi?"

"Oh, that!" I said.

How could I forget that? One night, our family went to a sushi restaurant on Columbus Avenue for my aunt Maxine's birthday. I'm not a big fan of raw fish myself, but all the grown-ups ordered a huge platter of sushi. On the corner of the platter there was a little pile of stuff that looked like green mustard. I love mustard, so I took one of my chopsticks and put a smidge of the green stuff on the end. It didn't smell like anything bad, so I popped it in my mouth. Let me tell you this: The minute that stuff hit my tongue, I thought my face was on fire. That tiny speck of green horseradish was so spicy, I was sure my whole nose was going to fly off my face and go running all the way to Central Park and jump in the pond to cool off.

I looked at the jar of red chili powder in our cart.

"If this stuff is anything like that wasabi, then maybe we should forget about the zing," I said.

"Hankie, live a little," Papa Pete said. "You need a dash of spice in your enchiladas. Otherwise they wouldn't be enchiladas."

"You mean schmintzaladas," Frankie said.

We all cracked up, even Papa Pete.

We were all still laughing when we left Gristediano's and headed home.

CHAPTER 14

MY MOM MUST HAVE ALERTED the entire apartment building that we were having a special visitor. When we turned the corner onto our block, I could see most of our neighbors standing under our green awning, waiting to say hello to Yoshi. There were so many of them, for a minute I thought they were welcoming the president of Japan and not just a fourth-grader like me.

Frankie's parents were there, and Ashley's, too. Her grandmother, who lives with them, was holding a plate of steamed pork dumplings. She probably thought we needed a backup in case my mom made one of her usual experimental taste-free, mock-tuna-filled dinners.

Good thinking, Grandma Wong!

As we got closer to our building, I could see Mrs. Park, who lives on the fourth floor, yelling at Mr. Grasso, who's right above her on the fifth floor. She always complains that he leaves his TV on too loud at night. Little Tyler King, who lives with his mom on our floor, was dressed for bed in his Spider-Man pajamas and Elmo slippers. I just love little kids in their pajamas. They're so squeezable, like baby koala bears—although I've never actually squeezed one of those. I'd like to, though.

My mom and dad were there, waving at us like lunatics. Our next-door neighbor, Mrs. Fink, was there, too. I like her, even though she almost never wears her false teeth and you can see her pink gums when she smiles. She has a crush on Papa Pete, but he doesn't have a crush back on her. I'm pretty sure that's because of the no-teeth problem I just mentioned.

"Peter!" Mrs. Fink called out when she saw us coming. "I'm over here."

Papa Pete handed me the bag of groceries.

"You carry these, Hankie," he said. "I'm taking off before she invites me up for her poppy seed upside-down sponge cake. Everything she bakes is cockeyed."

"You can't leave," I said to him. "You need to help us make the enchiladas."

"Hankie," Papa Pete said, taking my face in his hands. "I would fly to the moon for you. I would pluck a star out of the sky for you. I would catch a whale with my teeth for you. But I'm sorry, darling boy, I cannot spend another evening watching Mrs. Fink gum her poppy seed cake into mush."

"Look on the bright side, Papa Pete," Frankie said. "At least none of the poppy seeds gets stuck in her teeth."

"I need you to back me up on this, young man," Papa Pete said to Frankie. "You have all the ingredients you need. And I'm sure you kids can find a recipe for cheese enchiladas somewhere."

"Mom has hundreds of cookbooks," Emily said.

"No, I meant with real cheese, not soy cheese," Papa Pete said. "Maybe try the Internet."

"I'm quite good at research, if I do say so myself," said Robert, puffing up his skinny little chest at Emily, who couldn't take her eyes off Yoshi.

"We'll be fine, Papa Pete," Emily said. Easy

for her to say—she wasn't the one bringing in the enchiladas for the whole school to eat.

"Just be careful your mother doesn't slip any mung beans in when you're not looking," Papa Pete warned.

Mrs. Fink had taken a white handkerchief out of her sleeve and was waving it at Papa Pete. He went into a whole big pantomime, pointing to his watch like he was really late for something. Quickly, he kissed Emily and me on the heads, and pinched Frankie, Yoshi, and yes, even the cheekless wonder, Robert. Then he took off down Amsterdam Avenue like a bolt of lightning.

"*Ojiisan* is cool," Yoshi said. "I like your family, Hank."

Emily grinned at Yoshi with that same goofy smile she'd had all afternoon.

"Don't get carried away," I whispered to her. "I'm sure he wasn't talking about you."

"How do you know?" she snapped.

"Fourth-graders know these things."

"Yeah," Robert piped up, his nasal voice cracking really badly. "We do."

"Yoo-hoo, little man," Frankie said to

Robert. "You're in the third grade."

"But not for long," Robert said. He had a point there.

Cheerio was on a leash, standing next to my dad. The minute he saw us walking toward them, he went completely nuts. He's already pretty nuts, so he didn't have far to go. He started spinning in circles around my dad's legs until my dad was all wrapped up in his leash like one of those old Egyptian mummies.

My mom had to undo the leash to get my dad untangled, so Cheerio took off and came running to us. He sniffed at Yoshi, then started nipping at his ankles. That's what he does when he likes someone. Yoshi bent down to pet him, and Cheerio licked his face like it was a liver-flavored doggy biscuit. Boy, if Ms. Adolf could have seen my little Cheerio with Yoshi, she'd take back what she had said about him being dangerous. He is without a doubt the sweetest dog on four short legs.

Finally, after saying hello to everyone in the apartment, we were able to get into the elevator and ride up to the tenth floor, which is where we live. My mom unlocked our apartment door, and we all went into the living room. Everyone but Yoshi, that is. I stuck my head back out in the hall and saw him sitting on the floor, taking his shoes off.

"You get mud on your feet or something?" I asked him.

"In Japan, we take our shoes off before coming into the house," he said. "It's a sign of respect."

Boy, did I feel like an idiot, multi-culturally speaking.

There wasn't time for me to be embarrassed, though. The Zipzers had zipped into action. Everyone in my family wanted a piece of Yoshi, and he was being pulled in a million different directions.

My dad nabbed him first and showed him his mechanical pencil collection.

"*Ikeru,*" Yoshi said, politely touching a couple of the shiny silver pencils.

My dad broke into a big smile.

"*Ikeru,*" he repeated. "A five-letter word meaning 'It's good!' in Japanese. That was in my crossword puzzle last week and I missed it! Thank you, Yoshi!"

If you're Stanley Zipzer, life just doesn't get any better than that.

While my dad was demonstrating to Yoshi how you change the lead in a mechanical pencil, my mom kept interrupting.

"Feel free to use the bathroom anytime," she told Yoshi about a million times. I knew she really wanted him to check out the new wallpaper she had put up. I think she was very proud of it. It was yellow, with green pagodas.

Emily dragged Yoshi into her room to meet Katherine, who didn't even hiss at him. She didn't look at him, either. I think Old Kathy was still recovering from being glued down to the kitchen floor. A thing like that has got to affect you, even if you are a lower life-form.

To make the evening totally perfect, my mom even made a good dinner. Well, that's because she didn't really make it. She picked it up from the deli. Vlady put together an assortment of mile-high sandwiches for us—roast beef, pastrami, chicken salad, and turkey with Swiss. There was enough for Frankie and Ashley and Robert to come, too.

"What are you children going to do after

dinner?" my mom asked.

"Homework," I answered.

"I'm dreaming," Emily said. "Hank Zipzer is going to do his homework. No way."

"Maybe Hank is turning over a new leaf," my dad said. He loves that expression. Every time I get a really, really bad grade like a D on my report card, which is every time I get a report card, he tells me it's time to turn over a new leaf. I've turned over so many new leaves, my tree is almost naked. By the time I get to sixth grade, that tree will be completely bare.

"We're going to make enchiladas," I announced to one and all.

"You just said you were going to do homework," my dad pointed out.

"This is our homework, Dad. We're supposed to bring in a dish for the Multi-Cultural Lunch. Our group has decided to bring enchiladas."

"Oh, I have a lovely recipe for enchiladas with mung beans," my mom said.

I was in the middle of taking a sip of apple juice. When I heard the words *mung beans*, I burst out laughing and sprayed poor Robert all over the front of his white shirt. Even though I accidentally sprayed some of the apple juice on our new place mats, too, no one got mad at me. Not even my dad. We were all just in a great mood. In fact, if you had been standing outside our apartment and listening, all you would have heard was the sound of us laughing.

Oh, yeah, and my mom saying, "Yoshi, feel free to use the bathroom anytime."

CHAPTER 15

IT DIDN'T TAKE US LONG to find an enchilada recipe. Robert found a site that had seventy-two of them. We chose Mama Vita's Killer Cheesy Enchiladas. The recipe was the sixty-seventh one on Mama Vita's Killer Recipe site, right in between her Killer Shrimp Burritos and her Killer Pinto Bean Soup. Personally, I didn't know how anything involving pinto beans can be killer. If you ask me, they're like wet paste that sticks to the roof of your mouth.

After we decided on which recipe we were going to make, we printed it out and called Papa Pete. He thought it sounded fine, so we were good to go. My mom said we could be alone in the kitchen as long as we called her when it was time to turn the stove on.

"I know where the pots and pans are," Emily said, who was trying to impress Yoshi and act like she cooked all the time.

We all started digging through the cupboards. I pulled out a frying pan. Frankie was reaching for another pot and got shoved by Robert, who stepped on my frying pan. He went sliding across the kitchen floor like he was on a snowboard.

"Attention, everyone," Ashley said, getting out a wooden spoon and tapping it against the countertop like she was a judge in a courtroom. "This isn't working. We need to get organized."

Ashley is great at running things. Frankie and Ashley and I have a magic act called Magik 3. Frankie is the magician, and we made Ashley our manager. It was one of the smartest things we've ever done. She's so good at it, she managed us right into earning a grand total of $58.60. And we're not even out of fourth grade yet!

"For starters, everyone can't do the same job," Ashley said.

"Good thinking, Ashweena," Frankie said with a nod. "I'll put together all the ingredients."

"Great. Hank, you read Frankie the recipe and tell him what he needs," Ashley said.

"I'll do my best," I said.

It wasn't the best job for me to get, since

reading isn't exactly my strong point, but I didn't want to announce that in front of Yoshi.

"What should I do?" Robert asked.

"Disappear?" Frankie suggested.

"Okay," said Robert. "I'm only in third grade, anyway." He went into the living room to help my dad work a crossword puzzle.

"Emily, you and Yoshi can be the assistant chefs," said Ashley.

Ordinarily Emily would have thrown a hissy fit to be the assistant anything, but she was just happy to be next to Yoshi.

I was glad to see that Ashley was acting like herself again. One lovey-dovey girl in a kitchen was plenty for me. I guess Ashley saw how stupid Emily looked staring at Yoshi with her goo-goo eyes, and decided to call it quits. Ashley isn't the goo-goo-eye type, thank goodness.

"What are you going to do, Ash?" Frankie asked. "You can't just stand there and manage."

"I'm going to be the director," she said.

She disappeared through the swinging door and came back a second later, holding her dad's video camera.

"This is Ashley Wong, reporting for the

Zipzer Cooking Channel," she said, turning the camera on. "Our special guest tonight is Yoshi Morimoto. Yoshi, what do you have to say to your friends back home?"

"Cowabunga, dudes," Yoshi said, grinning into the camera.

"Thank you for your words of wisdom," Ashley said.

"Ash, why are you videotaping this?" I asked her.

"We want Yoshi to remember us, don't we? When he looks at this tape, he can see us whenever he wants."

See what I mean about Ashley being a good manager? She thinks of everything, even before it happens. I wish I could do that.

"Okay, I'm ready to roll," Frankie said. "Lay it on me, Zipola."

"Translation, please, Frankola."

"Read me the ingredients, dude. I'm ready to cook up a storm."

I propped the recipe page up on the counter, holding it upright with two cans of tomato sauce and a jar of Papa Pete's pickles.

"Twelve corn tortillas," I began, reading off

the first ingredient listed.

Truthfully, I couldn't read the word *tortilla*, but there was a picture on the page of Mama Vita's hands rolling up what looked like a tortilla, so I guessed that's what the word was. I do that a lot when I can't actually read something. You might call it guessing, but I like to call it figuring it out. Anytime I can figure out a word on my own and not have to ask someone, it saves me from being embarrassed one more time. By the way, shouldn't *tortilla* be spelled TOR-TEE-YA? Where did all those L's come from?

"Twelve tortillas. Check," Frankie said, tearing open the plastic bag and spreading the tortillas out on the counter.

"Three cups of shredded cheese," I said.

"Cheese, Louise," said Frankie. "Check."

It took a little time for Emily to grate the cheese into shreds. Every two seconds she kept saying, "Oh, I nicked my knuckle. Oh, I nicked it again." When it was finally done, Frankie put a handful of cheese into each tortilla. Yoshi and Emily helped him roll them up so the cheese stayed inside.

"What's next?" Frankie asked.

"One can of tomato sauce," I said.

"Check," Frankie said. He handed Yoshi the can opener and the tomato sauce.

"Get busy, Yosh my man," he said.

"Check, Frankie-*san*," answered Yoshi.

"Emily, stop staring at Yoshi and look up here at the camera," Ashley said. "Say something you want Yoshi to remember."

Emily put her hand over her mouth and started to giggle. I don't think I've ever heard her giggle. Correction. She once giggled in the pet store when George who works there told her she could feed a live mouse to the snake. Yup, that's what the girl giggled at, all right.

"What's next, Zip?"

"Chili powder," I said. "You're supposed to mix it into the tomato sauce."

"Oh right, for zing," Frankie said. "How much, my man?"

I looked back up at the recipe page in front of me. There were a lot of words on that page. The chili powder was way down at the bottom of a long list of ingredients.

Don't tell me. Could that be a fraction? No,

please don't be a fraction. You know how I feel about them.

Ashley turned the camera on me.

"Come on, Hank," she said. "Let the camera have it. With feeling. How much chili powder?"

"Uh, let's see." I squinted at the page. I could feel myself getting confused.

What does that stupid little line in the middle of the numbers mean? Face it, Hank. You don't have a clue.

I stared at the numbers next to the words *chili powder*. There was a *one* and a *three* and a little black line floating around somewhere in the middle of them. I was getting nervous, which happens to me when I know I don't know what I'm supposed to know. The type on the page was all starting to swim all over the page, like it had a mind of its own.

Maybe it isn't a fraction at all. Maybe that line is just a smudge on the paper. Or a little bug that flew in there and got squished.

"How much chili powder, dude?" I heard Frankie saying. "The tomato sauce is getting lonely."

I looked up and saw the camera on me.

"Speak up," Ashley shouted. "We're rolling!"

Yoshi was taking this tape back to Japan. He was going to watch it with all his friends there. And what were they going to see? Me, Hank Zipzer, boy moron. They were going to see me make a stupid mistake on a stupid fraction because I'm too stupid to figure out how much chili powder we needed!

Don't do this to me, brain. Fire up! Kick in! How much chili powder? Just read the number. Please, help me out here!

There was nothing cooking in my head. The only thing I could think was that I didn't want Yoshi to remember me as the kid who had to ask what a fraction was. But I had no choice.

I turned to the camera and was about to speak when—

"Watch out!" Emily yelled.

Her voice startled me back into reality. I jumped so high, I thought I was going to hit my head on the ceiling.

"What? Watch out for what?" I screamed.

"Kathy! She's under your feet."

I looked down and there she was again. Katherine, the lovely lizard, was darting across the room and making a run for the open cupboard where we keep the pots and pans.

"This is great!" Ashley said, turning the video camera from me to Katherine. "An action scene!"

Katherine dove into the cupboard and banged around in the pasta pots. I guess she wasn't a fan of Italian cooking, because she was out of there in a flash. I'll bet she saw her reflection in one of the pans and scared herself silly. She scurried across the kitchen floor, practically leaping from the refrigerator to the stove and back again. She must have been having a flashback to that afternoon and her linoleum nightmare, because let me tell you, she was one freaked-out lizard.

Emily ran after her, waving her arms and chasing her around the kitchen. Ashley followed with the video camera.

"A director's dream!" she shouted. "A chase sequence!"

This was my chance. The camera was off me, and no one was looking. I picked up a spoon and grabbed the jar of chili powder. I looked at the recipe book one more time. What did it say? Maybe this time I'd get it!

Is it three spoonfuls? Or one third? Or one thirty-third? Or thirty-three one hundredths?

I pushed the spoon deep into the chili powder and dug out a heaping pile of the bright red spice. I threw it into the tomato sauce. It didn't look like enough to me, so I threw in another heaping spoonful. Then I added a few pinches more with my fingers, just like I had always seen my mother do.

There, that looks right to me. I don't know how much I put in—it was something involving a three. Close enough.

By this time, Katherine had dashed back into the cupboard and was hiding behind the omelet pan. Emily started to cry.

"Don't be scared, Kathy," she said. "Mama's here."

Katherine was all out of breath. She just stared at us with her beady little eyes. When Emily tried to reach for her, she hissed and poked her long tongue out. She wasn't coming out of there for anyone anytime soon.

That is, until Robert showed up.

He had come in from the living room with my mom and dad when they heard the commotion.

"Let me try to get her," Robert said. "I have a way with the reptile kingdom."

Robert got down on his hands and knees in front of Katherine. He stuck his tongue out at her, and I swear, the two of them looked alike. Except Robert didn't have a tail. At least, none that I knew of.

Robert and Katherine continued their weird communication for what seemed like way too long for me. Then he started to make strange sounds in his throat. Iguana sounds.

"Coo roo ca ca shoo," he said. "Coo roo ca ca shoo."

What did that mean—"Get out of there right now, you scaly beast!"?

Katherine blinked her eyes and stared at Robert. As a matter of fact, we were all staring at Robert, Yoshi especially. I hoped he wasn't thinking that this was a typical night in a typical American family. Even for the Zipzers, this was extraordinary.

"Coo roo ca ca shoo," Robert repeated softly. He stuck his tongue out a couple more times. Then, slowly, he reached into the cupboard and picked up Katherine. She didn't do anything. She seemed really peaceful as she snuggled up against his bony chest. Maybe she thought she was leaning against tree roots.

"She's safe now," he whispered to Emily.

"Oh, Robert," Emily said with a sigh. "You saved her."

Emily was so happy, she reached out and gave Robert a kiss. I'm not going to describe it, because why gross all of us out? It's bad enough I had to see it with my own eyes. But I will tell you this: Robert turned bright red from his ears to his fingertips. He was as red as . . . well . . . chili powder.

Robert stood up, still holding Katherine.

"I'll go put her in her cage," he said. "She's had a hard thirty minutes."

They practically floated out of the kitchen. Just a boy, a girl, and a blissed-out reptile.

I looked over at Yoshi. He gave me a thumbs-up, and I could see how relieved he was. Wouldn't you be if my sister Emily fell out of love with you? She fell out of love so hard, you could almost see her hit the floor.

CHAPTER 16

"I can't believe I got all that on video-tape," Ashley said. "The cooking show is going to seem pretty dull after the Big Kiss."

"Can we not talk about that ever again, Ash?" I groaned.

"I'm with you on that one, Ziparooney," said Frankie. "Some things are meant to be forgotten, and I'm pushing that K-I-S-S out of my brain as fast as I can. Now where were we?"

"Zing," said Yoshi.

"Good thinking, Yosh Man," Frankie said. "Hankster was just about to tell me how much chili powder to put in the enchilada sauce."

"I already put it in," I said, saying a silent thank-you to Katherine for saving me.

"How much did you put in?" Frankie wanted to know.

"Just the right amount. The amount couldn't be more perfect."

"And how much was that?" Ashley asked. "Not that we don't trust you, Hank."

"Hey, did I tell you how to shoot your video?" I asked her.

"No."

"Good. Then don't tell me how to cook my enchiladas."

"Have it your way," Ashley said with a shrug.

Now all I could do was hope that what I hoped was the right amount was *really* the right amount.

CHAPTER 17

PAPA PETE CALLED ME FIRST THING the next morning.

"I'm coming to pick you up to take you to school," he told me. "Your mother said you made a big pan of enchiladas. It's probably too heavy to carry."

"But, Papa Pete, you don't have a car," I pointed out.

"Hankie, why would something like that stop me?" he said, and hung up.

We waited for him outside our apartment. Frankie held my backpack while Yoshi and I balanced the pan of enchiladas between us. Robert and Emily were there, too, making goo-goo eyes at each other. After a few minutes, a long black limousine pulled up. I couldn't see who was in it because the windows were blacked out. I thought it was probably a movie star. Either that or a Met. I was wrong, though. It was Papa Pete! He is full of surprises.

When he rolled down the passenger window and asked if we needed a ride, I thought Yoshi's eyeballs were going to fall out of his head. Actually, I thought mine were, too. I had never ridden in a limousine in my life!

"Meet Dave Waxman," Papa Pete said, slapping the driver of the car on the back. "He's the second-best bowler on the Chopped Livers, after yours truly." Papa Pete's bowling team is called the Chopped Livers. They're first in their league. "When I told Dave about Yoshi, he volunteered to take him for a spin in this sweet little buggy of his."

"Thank you, *ojiisan*," said Yoshi. "You, too, Waxman-*san*."

"My pleasure, kiddo," said Dave. "Hop in."

We all climbed in the rear door of the limo. Inside, there was a telephone and neon lights, and smooth leather seats that felt like butter. It was so big in there that you could have played hide-and-seek, which by the way, we did. If you ever get a chance to ride in a limousine, I highly recommend playing hide-and-seek.

"I could drive all the way to Japan in this car," Ashley said.

Robert cleared his throat. "Actually, you couldn't, because Japan is—"

"We know, Robert," we all groaned. "An island country surrounded by water."

"Dude, don't you have any other topics?" Frankie asked.

"Actually, I could speak about the spiny tailed iguana of Costa Rica. It is the fastest reptile on the planet, able to run twenty-one miles per hour."

"Oh, Robert, you're so interesting," my geekoid sister said.

Attention! Calling all nerds! There's a meeting in the back of our limo!

It's only six blocks to my school, and we were really sorry our ride was so short. When we pulled up in front, we saw Yoshi's father waiting on the steps, talking to Ms. Adolf. Boy, were they shocked to see us get out of that car.

Yoshi gave his dad a hug and started blabbering to him in Japanese. I hoped he was talking about the limousine ride and not giving him an earful about Katherine's nervous breakdown in our kitchen last night.

Ms. Adolf gave me one of her nastier looks.

"What's the purpose of this vehicle? It is so extravagant," she said as the limo pulled away.

"Hmmm, the purpose." I thought it over. "It's a fun way to get somewhere?"

"Fun is not appropriate, Henry. I won't have my pupils just going about willy-nilly, having *fun* whenever they feel like it."

I had never heard the word *fun* sound so un-fun. I switched to a topic I thought she'd like better.

"We made enchiladas for the Multi-Cultural Day Lunch," I said, sticking the pan under her nose.

She looked into the pan like there were worms crawling around in there.

"They look extremely cheesy," she said. "Are they spicy?"

"They have a little zing," Ashley answered.

"Not too much zing, I hope," Ms. Adolf said. "I don't respond well to spicy Mexican food. I'm sure our guests don't, either. We don't want to make them sick."

That was a scary thought.

What if I put in too much chili powder? Will the enchiladas be too spicy? Will they make Yoshi sick? Will he go screaming out of the room, begging for water? Worse yet, what if they make Mr. Morimoto sick?

Stop it, Hank!

My thoughts were making me sick.

I looked at the enchiladas in the pan. Exactly how zingy were they? There was only one way to find out. I had to taste them.

CHAPTER 18

As THE BELL RANG and everyone went inside, Ms. Adolf told me to take the enchiladas to the Multi-Purpose Room. That gave me an idea. I'd put them down and, when no one was looking, take one little bite. If they were too spicy, I'd throw them out right then and there. At least that way I'd be sure I wasn't going to give the whole school a stomachache.

Frankie held the front door open for me.

"Frankie, Ashley, come along to class," Ms. Adolf said. She and her gray shoes were already halfway up the stairs. "It doesn't take all of you to deliver your tamales."

"They're enchiladas," I corrected her.

"Whatever."

Obviously, Ms. Adolf wasn't big on Mexican food. Probably because it wasn't gray.

"Are you sure you can make it there without

dropping the pan?" Frankie asked me.

I was wondering the same thing myself.

"Come along," Ms. Adolf said, pointing to the steps that led to our classroom.

"Put our dish where everyone can see it," Ashley whispered to me as she headed upstairs. "I think it looks delicious."

"It kicks butt," Yoshi said.

And then they were gone, leaving me alone with one heavy pan of killer cheesy enchiladas.

I hoped I wasn't going to have to throw them away. All my friends were counting on seeing our dish, front and center. How would I explain it if I had to throw it out?

Sorry, guys. Guess who couldn't read a recipe? That's right. Me.

Don't get me wrong. It's not like my friends wouldn't understand. Frankie and Ashley know all about my learning challenges, and they are very understanding. Ashley always helps me count out the right change when we stop at Harvey's to get a slice of pizza. And Frankie helps me in a million ways. He puts new toys together for me when I can't figure out the instruction booklets. He set up my e-mail when

I got my new computer. He even quizzes me on our spelling words when we walk to school.

But here's the part even Frankie and Ashley wouldn't understand: They wouldn't get why I just didn't say, "Stop the camera. I can't read the recipe." To them, that's not a big deal at all. But it is to me.

I don't think even my best friends really know what it feels like to be me. I hate feeling that I'm not as smart as other people. I hate feeling ashamed of myself all the time. And I hate that I can't count on my brain to get it right. Sure, Dr. Berger says there's nothing to be ashamed of, that we all learn differently and in our own time. But that's easy for her to say and very hard for me to believe. She isn't the one who has to say, "Stop the camera. I can't read."

I walked down the main hall toward the Multi-Purpose Room and past the trophy case. I noticed a picture of Principal Love right in the center of all our school trophies. Don't ask me why it was there. You sure wouldn't want to win him in a game.

I passed the attendance office, where Mrs. Crock was sitting at her desk, squinting at her computer screen.

"Hi, Hank," she called out. "What do you have there?"

"Cheese enchiladas. For Multi-Cultural Day."

"Isn't it yummy to be multi-cultural?" she said.

Wow, she was in a good mood. In fact, everybody I passed in the hall was, too. There was a feeling of a party in the air. The kids in the kindergarten room were busy making paper plates into African masks.

"I'm going to dance at the lunch today," one of the little guys said as I passed by. "Wanna see?"

He burst into a wild and crazy dance, shaking his butt and making up weird steps as he went along. I remember doing that in kindergarten. Frankie and I danced like total goofballs in front of the whole school, and we weren't ashamed or embarrassed even a little bit. Those were the good old days.

By the time I reached the Multi-Purpose Room, I was dying to put down the pan of enchiladas. It's a long hallway, and my arms were aching. The first person I saw was Mr. Rock. He was on a stepladder, hanging the welcome sign we had made for Yoshi. I noticed Ashley's pink rhinestones on the sign, sparkling out at me like cherry blossoms.

"Hi, Hank. That's a mighty big load you're carrying," Mr. Rock said.

"I didn't know enchiladas were so heavy," I answered.

"Here, let me give you a hand with that," Mr. Rock said, hopping off the ladder. Before I could object, he had grabbed the pan from my hands.

"You make these yourself?" he asked.

"A bunch of us made them together," I said.

"Well, since these were made by kids for kids, I think they should go right in the middle," he said, plopping them down smack in the center of the table.

I was hoping to slide the enchiladas onto a side table so I could sneak a bite without anyone noticing. This center table development put a minor wrinkle in my plans, but I could deal with it. Mr. Rock would go back to his sign hanging in a minute, and I'd creep over there and grab my test taste.

Squeak, squeak, squeak.

Oh, no. There's only one person in school whose shoes squeak like that. And that person could put a major wrinkle in my plan.

"Well, well, well. If it isn't Mr. Zipzer," said a tall man, bushy haired voice.

I turned around and there they were—the three of them: Principal Love, his hairy blue and yellow scarf, and his mole. They all looked happy to see me. I was not happy to see them.

"Mr. Morimoto reported that his son had an excellent evening last night," he said. "Good job, young man."

"Thank you, sir."

Could you leave now? Please?

"Remember this, Mr. Zipzer, because I'm not going to say it twice. We build bridges between people so boats can sail under them."

I counted to ten, waiting.

"Yes, siree," he repeated, right on schedule. "We build bridges between people so boats can sail under them. Do you understand, Mr. Zipzer?"

"Yes, sir. Every word."

I did understand every word. I just didn't

understand what they meant when you put them all together.

"And might I inquire why you're here and not in class?" Principal Love asked me.

"We made a dish for the Multi-Cultural Day Lunch," I answered. "I was dropping it off."

"Hank contributed those fine-looking enchiladas there," Mr. Rock said.

"Ah, enchiladas," Principal Love said. "A delicious taste treat from south of the border. There is no such thing as a bad enchilada. No, siree. There is no such thing as a bad enchilada."

I hoped he was right about that. I was afraid that I had just cranked out a whole pan of really bad enchiladas.

"Now that your mission is accomplished, I'll take you back to your classroom," Principal Love said. "I was just heading there to check on young Mr. Morimoto."

"Oh, uh, th-thanks, sir, but I still have m-more to do here," I stammered.

"There's nothing for you to do here," said Principal Love. "None of the other dishes have even arrived yet."

"I'd like to stay," I said.

"And I'd like to ride a yak through Tibet," said Principal Love. "We can't always do what we like."

But I HAD to stay. I didn't have the chance to taste the enchiladas yet. My mission was not accomplished.

Principal Love was heading for the door. He stopped and waited for me to join him.

"I have to stay, sir."

"No, you don't. Now come with me right now."

Think of something, Hankster. Let your mouth do the talking.

"Sir, I really want to go back to class with you," I began, "but the reason I have to stay involves my friend Ashley Wong, who worked long and hard to glue all those pink rhinestones on that sign over there."

"What's that have to do with you?" Principal Love asked in a gruff voice. This wasn't going so well. I had to kick it up a notch.

"Well, sir," I whispered. "She asked if I could stand guard because—I don't mean to alarm you—but rhinestones have been disappearing from that sign in record numbers. We suspect two or three of the kindergarteners. Have you noticed how sparkly they have been lately?"

It wasn't my mouth's best work, but it was all I could come up with at the time.

"This is ridiculous," Principal Love said, rubbing his face with his hand. His index finger brushed across the Statue of Liberty, poking her somewhere between her rump and her armpit.

"I don't know what you're trying to do, young man, but I'm not going to let you do it. Come with me. I'm taking you back to class."

I looked over to Mr. Rock. Even he couldn't help me now.

CHAPTER 19

PRINCIPAL LOVE DROPPED ME OFF in Ms. Adolf's room and picked up Yoshi. He was taking him to spend the morning with the fifth-grade classes and then on an exciting tour of the library. Yoshi wasn't going to be back with us again until the buffet lunch.

I was stuck in class all morning. Three times I asked Ms. Adolf for a hall pass to go to the Multi-Purpose Room. Three times she said no.

She said I had to stay in my seat and work on our assignment. We had to write an in-class essay on Multi-Cultural Day. This is what mine said:

Multi-Cultural Day by Hank Zipzer

I hope I don't ruin it.

The End

CHAPTER 20

BECAUSE OUR CLASS WAS HOSTING the luncheon, we had to go to the Multi-Purpose Room a few minutes before lunchtime to make sure everything was all set up. I was nervous as we walked down the hallway. I knew it was too late to sneak our enchiladas out of there. The ship had sailed, as Papa Pete likes to say. There was nothing I could do now but hope they weren't going to be hotter than firecrackers.

Calm down, Hank. It's not like you put the whole jar of chili powder in the sauce. Okay, maybe you put a little too much in. Then again, maybe you didn't. I hate that I don't know.

Most of me truly believed the enchiladas were going to be okay. I just wished I could get all of me to believe that.

When we walked into the Multi-Purpose Room, I was completely blown away. Wow, did it look different from how it had early in the morning.

It was wall-to-wall food. There were probably twenty tables set up, covered with tastes from all parts of the globe. Next to each dish was a sign explaining where it came from. Kidney pie from England. Squid floating in its own ink from Spain. I wondered if you ate it with a fountain pen. Puffy bread called naan from India. Olives from Greece. Bird's nest soup from China— without the bird of course. And our very own, very cheesy Killer Cheese Enchiladas from Mexico. Next to them were pigs in a blanket from Kansas. I think we all know what fool brought those in.

Good old Nick McKelty. He still thought Kansas was a foreign country near Brazil.

The room was an amazing sight. This wasn't just a multi-cultural lunch. It was a multi-multi-multi-cultural lunch. There was food from countries I hadn't even heard of, like Tonga and Burundi, and it was so colorful. Red and green and chocolate brown sauces were practically waving at you, saying, "Come on, try me. I'm delicious!"

"Look! Snails!" shouted Luke Whitman about two seconds after we had walked in.

He found them first thing, like a heat-seeking missile. They were over by the crepes filled with apricot jelly from France. A whole plate of snails, just lying around in their shells, with some butter and garlic and parsley on top. Wouldn't you know Captain Disgusto would grab one and pop it into his mouth, shell and all? The crunching sound was so loud, everyone in the room stopped talking.

"This tastes awesome," Luke said, spitting bits of shell out into his hand. "But they could use a little more slime."

"Eeuuww," Katie and Kim screamed. They went running over to the cake and pie section, which they were sure would be a slime-free zone.

Our enchiladas were still right there in the center of the main table. I could see that there was steam rising up from the pan and the cheese was all nice and melted. One of the room parents must have warmed them up while we were in class.

Ms. Adolf had told us to wander around the room and arrange all the dishes nicely on the table. She was doing the same thing herself. At least, that's what she was pretending to do. I noticed that she was sampling a taste here and there. She wasn't fooling me. I saw her pop that Greek olive in her mouth, and swipe a sweet-and-sour shrimp.

"Look, there's the Yosh Man," Frankie said, pointing across the room.

Yoshi was just entering the room, with Principal Love on one side of him and his dad on the other. He looked like he was asleep on his feet. Obviously, the library tour hadn't been all that exciting for him. So many books and so hard to read.

When he saw us, his face lit up.

"Cowabunga, dudes," he hollered from across the room.

"Why don't you jerks teach him something new to say?" Nick McKelty shouted. "He's getting annoying."

If anyone would know anything about being annoying, it would be Nick the Tick. He was the master, the commander, the prince of annoying.

Frankie, Ashley, and I ignored McKelty and went to say hi to Yoshi.

"Hey, Yoshi, you've got to see our

enchiladas," Ashley said. "They're over there on the center table."

"Ah, enchiladas," Mr. Morimoto said. "Yoshi and I love them. I'll have to taste one."

I wished I knew how to say, "I'd think twice about that if I were you," in Japanese, but since I didn't, I just smiled and said, *"Ikeru, Morimoto-san."*

"Oh, you speak Japanese." Mr. Morimoto smiled. He turned to Principal Love. "This is a very impressive young man."

"That he is. That he is," Principal Love said, giving me a friendly slap on the back. I was so unprepared for his sudden display of affection that I almost fell over into Ryan Shimozato's beef sukiyaki.

Suddenly, we heard a commotion coming from the center of the room, near the table with our enchiladas. Several of the parents had gathered in a circle, surrounding someone.

"Step away, and give her some air," one of them was saying.

When the parents moved away, we saw who it was they were surrounding.

Ms. Adolf!

Oh, she didn't look good. Not that she ever looks good, but at that moment, she looked especially not good. Her face was turning bright red. I had never seen color in her face before.

The next thing we knew, Ms. Adolf let out a noise that wasn't like any human sound I had ever heard. It was somewhere between a cough and a hiss and a gasp.

"Water!" she hissed. "Get me water!"

She sounded like Golem in *The Lord of the Rings*. She was hissing pretty loudly, and her face looked like a tomato about to explode. Then she started hopping around the room, like a kangaroo with its feet on fire.

"You go, girlfriend," Frankie whispered under his breath as he watched her hop.

Ashley burst out laughing. I didn't want to laugh, so I just concentrated on smiling very, very hard. Sometimes that keeps the laugh inside.

"What happened to that poor woman?" Mr. Morimoto asked.

"Must have been something she ate," Principal Love said. Then he turned and looked directly at me. "I hope it wasn't your enchiladas."

That wiped the smile off my face really fast. "No, sir," I said. "Like you always say, there's no such thing as a bad enchilada, sir."

Man, oh, man. If only that were true.

Ms. Adolf grabbed an ice cube from the punch bowl and rubbed it all over her tongue. Then she rubbed it on her face, too, eyebrows and all. Then it went back on her tongue again. Face. Tongue. Face. Tongue. She couldn't slide that cube around fast enough. And then her face started to drip.

Ashley had tears in the corners of her eyes. That happens to her when she's dying to laugh but has to hold it in.

As I watched Ms. Adolf mambo around the room, I started to think how interesting it was that she had been standing right next to our pan of enchiladas when her tongue attacked her. I wasn't the only one to be thinking about that little fact. Frankie shot me a suspicious look.

"How much chili powder did you put in, dude?" he whispered to me.

"I told you," I whispered back. "The absolute right amount."

By now, Ms. Adolf's tongue was hanging out

of her mouth. She looked like Cheerio after he's gone for a long run in the park. She was leaping around the room, fanning her tongue with her hands.

"Are you all right?" Ryan Shimozato's mom asked her.

"Shiiicy," Ms. Adolf panted.

"What?" asked Ms. Shimozato. "I'm sorry, but I can't understand you."

In case you've never noticed, it's hard to understand people who are talking with their tongues hanging out of their mouths.

"Spicy!" Ms. Adolf screeched. She had shoved her tongue back in her mouth long enough to say that one word. Then, with two fingers, she grabbed the tip and pulled her tongue back out into the air and started fanning it with her gray silk scarf.

"I think she ate something too spicy," Ms. Shimozato said to the group of people who were standing around.

Frankie looked over at me and raised an eyebrow.

But before he could say anything, Ms. Adolf started to do this thing like she was whistling, but instead of blowing air out, she was sucking it in. That was followed by these horribly loud grunts, like my dad makes when he snores. A bunch of kids burst out laughing. It wasn't the nicest thing to do, but if you were there, you would have been laughing, too. I promise.

Ms. Adolf got a really weird look on her face. She came to a full stop. What was going to happen now? *Whoosh!* Suddenly, she started to move across the floor, wiggling her rump like she was doing the tango.

I don't know how to tell you what happened next without using the fart word. So let me say it this way. Ms. Adolf propelled herself across the Multi-Purpose Room as if she had a rocket in her skirt. And there was a certain sound that went along with that move. Once again, I can only refer you to the fart word.

"Eeuuww," Katie and Kim screamed. "Gross."

"Watch out, she's letting loose another one," Luke Whitman cried out as Ms. Adolf came shooting across the floor in the opposite direction. One hand was on her stomach, and the other was covering her mouth. As she flew by me, I thought I heard her say, "Oh, excuse me. I'm so sorry."

"Let's get you to the ladies' room," Ms. Shimozato said to Ms. Adolf. Ms. Adolf just nodded. We could hear her erupting as she was led off to the bathroom.

Frankie gave me The Look.

"Zip," he whispered. "Now I've *got* to know. You have to come clean about the chili powder."

"See, there was this fraction in the recipe—or at least I think it was a fraction—and I couldn't exactly tell if—"

"Zip, talk to me."

"I'm trying. I couldn't read the recipe," I answered honestly. "So I guessed. But it didn't seem like that much. Just enough to give the enchiladas a little zing."

"A little zing!" Frankie said. "Did you see Ms. Adolf, dude? It looked to me like she had enough zing to dance down to the Brooklyn Bridge. It sounded like it, too."

"What do we do now?" I asked. I was starting to feel embarrassed about the whole situation.

"Now that's a good question," Frankie said. "I just wish I knew the answer."

CHAPTER 21

WE ALL HUNG AROUND waiting to see if Ms. Adolf was going to explode through the ladies' room door.

"Attention, everyone," Ms. Shimozato said when she finally walked back into the Multi-Purpose Room. "I'm happy to report that Ms. Adolf is feeling much better. She has a delicate stomach and had a little reaction to something she ate."

"If that was a little reaction, I'd hate to smell a big one," McKelty laughed.

He was stuffing black forest cake from Germany into his mouth that was as big as the whole country of Germany. When he laughed, you could see the frosting shoot out from between his big front teeth. It landed everywhere, including on his dad, who had made the mistake of standing too close to hir

"She wants you all to go on and enjoy your-selves," Ms. Shimozato said. "She'll be back with us soon. She's just recovering in the . . . uh . . . uh . . . well, she's just recovering."

The adults in the room sighed with relief and went back to the buffet. A bunch of kids started to giggle. I mean, you can't hear about your teacher kicking back in the restroom and not find that funny, can you?

"Well, where were we?" Principal Love asked, turning to Mr. Morimoto.

"I was just about to help myself to one of those delicious enchiladas," Mr. Morimoto answered. "Come on, Yoshi, let's get one before they're gone."

Before I could say a word, Mr. Morimoto was heading over to the center table. Yoshi and Ashley were right behind him.

"He can't eat those," I said to Frankie.

"You know what you have to do," Frankie said.

"What should I tell him?"

"You'll come up with something, Ziparooney. You've got ten seconds and counting."

I went charging after Mr. Morimoto. He had

taken a paper plate and handed another one to Yoshi. They were already at the enchilada pan.

"Excuse me, sir," I said to him. "But may I suggest you try the squid in its own ink? Or how about a plump, tender snail swimming in buttery snail juice?"

"Perhaps later, Hank," Mr. Morimoto said. "My mouth is watering for a nice, spicy enchilada. It's not easy to find good Mexican food in Tokyo."

There's the good kind of spicy. And then there's the get-me-to-the-hospital-because-my-mouth-all-the-way-to-my-stomach-is-on-fire kind of spicy. Our enchiladas were in the second category for sure.

What if they make Mr. Morimoto sick and he winds up in the hospital? No, Hank. That can't happen. Stand up! Be a man!

I had no choice. I had to stop Mr. Morimoto from eating the enchilada. Period. End of thought. And that meant telling him the truth: that I dumped in too much chili powder because I couldn't read the stupid recipe.

Why can't my learning differences just go away, vanish like the magic scarves Frankie makes disappear up his sleeve?

Suddenly, there was Frankie at my side, standing next to me like always in times of trouble. He took me by the arm and pulled me far enough away so we could talk in private.

"Let's just go tell Mr. Morimoto the truth, Zip."

I don't want to! I hate the truth!

"He's a cool guy. He'll understand."

That's not the point. I don't want to feel stupid in front of everyone . . . again.

"You've got to tell him now, dude. Check it out. He's already got the enchilada on the serving fork."

I can come up with another reason why Mr. Morimoto shouldn't eat that enchilada. I know I can!

"Let's go, Zip. Now."

Think, Hank, think!

CHAPTER 22

TEN REASONS WHY MR. MORIMOTO SHOULD _NOT_ EAT THAT ENCHILADA

By Hank Zipzer

1. In America, it is considered extremely rude to eat red and yellow foods on Thursday.
2. It's a little known fact that chewing chili powder will make you go bald.
3. This is National Don't Eat Foods Beginning with "E" month.
4. That enchilada is the earth home of a band of miniature alien beings. I know this because I saw their spaceship land in the cheese.
5. Luke Whitman has already licked them with his snail-slime tongue.

6. Many people are allergic to enchilada juice. If they eat it, their bottom lips blow up, fall off, and try to find Mexico.
7. Yikes! I'm out of time. Mr. Morimoto is about to take the first bite! Mr. Morimoto! Stop! Stop!

CHAPTER 23

"STOP!" I SHOUTED OUT LOUD.

Incoming! Mr. Morimoto's mouth was open, and the enchilada-filled fork was heading into it.

"Wait!" I hollered, just before the fork touched his lips. "Don't eat that enchilada."

It seemed like everyone in the Multi-Purpose Room got quiet and turned their eyes on me.

"What's your problem, Zipper Boy?" said Nick McKelty. "You put rat tails in those enchiladas?"

"I think I put in too much chili powder," I said, hating to admit it but knowing I had to. "When Ms. Adolf got sick a few minutes ago, that was all my fault."

"How was it your fault, dear?" asked Ms. Shimozato.

"I wasn't sure how much chili powder to put in," I said. "So I put in a pinch. Then another.

137

And another."

"That sounds fine, dear," said Ms. Shimozato.

"It was. Until I put in a two more whole spoonfuls," I went on. "Then another pinch. Or three. Or four. Or five."

"Why didn't you follow the recipe, young man?" Principal Love asked.

There it was. The Big Question. I stared at his Statue of Liberty without the torch mole. Was she laughing at me? It sure looked like it.

The room got even quieter than before. Everyone was waiting for my answer. There was only one truthful answer to Principal Love's question: I didn't follow the recipe because I couldn't read it and I couldn't figure out what on earth that fraction meant.

But the other real truth was, my learning differences were not something I wanted to discuss right then in front of the whole world. I'm sure you wouldn't want to be chatting about your personal brain problems in front of a room full of people either. But everyone was waiting for my explanation, so I didn't really have a choice in the matter

I opened my mouth to answer, but nothing came out.

"Breathe, Zip," Frankie whispered to me. "Oxygen is power."

I took a deep breath, then spoke.

"To be honest, I had trouble reading the recipe," I said. There, at least I had begun.

Everyone in the room looked at one another and waited for me to go on. This was the part I was dreading. The fraction problem, the freak-out, the words floating across the page. Ick, ick, and triple ick.

I took another deep breath, but just as I started to talk, Mr. Rock popped up from the back of the room and came springing over to me. He threw his arm around my shoulder.

"I have trouble reading recipes, too," he said. "They get splattered with tomato sauce and smeared with butter and covered with brown gravy—and then you can't even read what's on the page. Cooking's a messy business, isn't it, Hank?"

All the grown-ups in the room nodded in agreement. Ms. Shimozato launched into a story about how she once splattered a whole pot of potato leek soup all over her cookbook when she forgot to put the top on the blender. Suddenly, no one was paying attention to me anymore.

Mr. Rock, you're a genius!

"Thank you," I whispered to him. "I really didn't want to go into the whole story."

"Your learning differences are your business, not theirs," whispered Mr. Rock. "You tell who you want to tell."

Just then, who do you think came strutting back into the room? Ms. Adolf! When she entered, everyone clapped. She smiled and took a little bow, as if getting a gas attack in public deserved a big round of applause. Her face wasn't red anymore. It was back to its original gray.

I knew I owed her an apology. I'm not a total idiot, you know.

"Ms. Adolf," I said. "I'm so sorry about the enchiladas."

"What do you have to be sorry about, Henry?"

"I'm sorry that they burned your mouth and made you sick," I said, carefully staying away from any mention of the gassy part of the attack. I thought that might embarrass her.

"They didn't make me sick," she said. "I never even tasted your enchiladas, although they did look surprisingly delicious."

"You didn't?"

"No, Henry. I told you earlier that the cuisine of Mexico does not sit well with me. It gives me gastric distress."

"What's she talking about?" Nick the Tick whispered to Luke Whitman.

"Mexican food makes her fart," Luke whispered back.

Nick nodded. "Copy that," he said.

"But if you didn't eat our enchiladas, then what made you sick?" I asked Ms. Adolf.

"It was the pigs in a blanket," she answered.

McKelty's dish! No way! This is the greatest thing ever! That big lug is going to have to take the fall for Ms. Adolf's gas attack. Oh, yeah! Life is good.

"Hey," McKelty protested. "There was nothing wrong with my pigs in a blanket. I made them myself."

"Well, Nicholas, it was right after I ate one

that I had my little problem," she said.

"It wasn't so little," muttered Luke.

"What did you put in your pigs in a blanket?" Ms. Adolf asked Nick.

"They're just cut-up hot dogs wrapped in a biscuit with mustard and a spoonful of horseradish," he answered.

"Horseradish!" Ms. Adolf said as if saying the word made her mouth burst into flames again. "Why, Nicholas McKelty, horseradish is incredibly spicy!"

"It is?" McKelty said. "Then why would they give it to horses?"

All the grown-ups started to chuckle. McKelty laughed, too. The jerk didn't even realize that they were laughing at him.

"Horseradish isn't for horses, Nicholas," said Ms. Adolf. "They call it horseradish because it is made from very large radishes."

"Actually, horseradish was bottled in the 1850s, making it one of the first convenience foods," said a nasal voice. It was Robert, the walking encyclopedia, joining the party in his usual fact-filled way. "Some native people as far back as the ancient Egyptians rubbed it on their foreheads to cure headaches," he added, in case he hadn't already been boring enough. "Others tossed it up into their armpits for bruised ribs."

I ask you, how in the world would any nine-year-old in his right mind know a thing like that? Even more mysterious is, why would he care?

"In Japan, we call horseradish wasabi and put it on our sushi," said Mr. Morimoto.

"Wasabi kicks butt," Yoshi said. "It is very spicy. It clears your nose."

"We know about that, don't we, Hank?" It was none other than Lizard Woman Emily, who had followed Robert into the room. "Hank was once personally attacked by a small pile of wasabi in a Japanese restaurant. He put up a good fight, though."

That was a decent thing for Emily to say. She could have told everyone that my nose had almost left my face, permanently looking for a sink filled with cold water—which was closer to the truth.

Nick McKelty can't stand it when anyone else gets a compliment of any kind. He always has to hog the attention for himself.

"That's nothing," he said, pulling himself up to his full humongous height. "Once, I ate the hottest chili pepper in the world. They say even a lick of it can kill you, but I chomped down ten of them, just like that."

"Right," Yoshi said. "And my name is Bernice."

Frankie reached out and gave Yoshi a high five.

"Way to go, Yosh Man," he said.

"Who is this Bernice?" asked Principal Love. "And why is everyone always talking about her?"

In case you hadn't noticed, Principal Love isn't too strong in the sense of humor department. Maybe he and Ms. Adolf are related.

"Many Japanese people enjoy spicy food," said Mr. Morimoto. "Personally, I find the spicier, the better."

I looked at Frankie and Ashley, and they looked back at me.

"Okay, Mr. M.," Frankie said. "If you're such a spice fan, have we got something for you."

The man said he liked spicy, and spicy was already on his plate.

"Dig right in to that enchilada," I said. "We

144

made it special for your taste buds."

Mr. Morimoto popped the first bite of enchilada into his mouth. He was quiet for a minute. Then his eyes started to tear up. His nose began to run. He took a handkerchief out of his pocket and blew his nose.

"Hank, may I have some water, please?" he said in a raspy voice.

Oh, no. I was frying the taste buds of the principal of a sister school from another country.

Mr. Morimoto took a sip of the water I brought him.

"This enchilada has a great deal of—I don't know how to say it in English," he said. He turned to Yoshi and said something in Japanese. Yoshi nodded.

"My father says this enchilada has a great deal of zing," Yoshi said.

"Is that good?" Principal Love asked.

"It's very good," Yoshi said. "Zing kicks butt."

I thought Principal Love was going to fall over on his face and crush the Statue of Liberty to bits. If one of us had said the words "kick butt" to him, he would have thrown us in detention for a week. But Yoshi could get away with it. What was Principal Love going to do? You don't put a guest from a faraway country into detention. That would be very rude, multi-culturally speaking.

Mr. Morimoto ate the whole enchilada. He drank a lot of water, too, and blew his nose after every bite. He ate two more enchiladas after that one. We had to get him an entire box of Kleenex.

"Thank you for an excellent meal," he said when he was finished. "That was most delicious."

"*Ikeru,*" Frankie said. "We had fun making it."

"Yeah, you can see it all on the video we made," Ashley said.

"I promise that Yoshi and I will play it for the children in my school," Mr. Morimoto said.

"They'll like the iguana part," Ashley said. "The lizard's got talent."

"Did you hear that, Robert?" Emily said. "Katherine's going to be an international TV star."

"Let's tell her all about it after school," Robert said.

I made a mental note to be sure to be really busy after school.

CHAPTER 24

THAT NIGHT, EVERYONE CAME OVER to our apartment for a party. As a way to say thank you, Yoshi gave me his silver sneakers, the ones that looked like they flew in from another galaxy. They were about three sizes too big, but I didn't care. Even if they were a little on the floppy side, they were still the coolest shoes I've ever seen. I used the old stuff-a-pair-of-socks-in-the-toe trick, and they were as good as mine.

I gave Yoshi my Mets sweatshirt to take back to Japan, although Frankie tried to get him to take his stinking Yankees sweatshirt instead. Can you believe that? Yoshi gave Frankie his Japanese rap CD. Frankie taught Yoshi the magic trick where you pull a nickel out of someone's ear.

"But we don't have nickels in Japan," Yoshi said.

"It will work with a yen, too, dude," Frankie said. "It's a very multi-cultural trick."

Ashley gave Yoshi a button she made that said *ikeru* in turquoise and yellow rhinestones. Yoshi gave her his chopsticks that had slivers of sparkly mother-of-pearl at the tips. He said it was okay if she wanted to add a few pink rhinestones of her own.

My mom cooked what she considered to be a typical American dinner, hamburgers and fries. Except that there was no meat, nothing fried—and, by the way, no taste either. Fortunately, we had all eaten so much at the Multi-Cultural Day Lunch that we weren't hungry. We offered Cheerio the leftovers, but he took one whiff, ran into the kitchen, and hid in the cupboard with the pasta pots. He must have learned that from Katherine. She was in Emily's room, going over her TV career plans with Robert and Emily. By the way, they asked Ashley if she wanted to be Katherine's manager, and she's considering it.

"Feel free to use the bathroom," my mom said to Mr. Morimoto about a thousand times during the evening. She was really happy when he finally did feel free to use it to wash his hands. And when he told her he thought the pagodas on the wallpaper were beautiful, I thought she was going to kiss him. Luckily, she kissed my dad instead, which was a good move on her part.

Speaking of my dad, I hadn't seen him that happy since he came in third in the tri-state crossword puzzle tournament in Jersey City. He showed Mr. Morimoto his mechanical pencil collection, of course. My dad has gotten used to people throwing a quick eyeball on his m.p.'s and then changing the subject as fast as they can. Most people have a limited interest in mechanical pencils and the thickness of the lead. You can't blame them. That's just the way it is.

But it turns out that Mr. Morimoto has a collection of floatie pens—those ballpoint pens that have water inside and little objects like boats and palm trees that float up and down in the bluish liquid. When my dad heard that, the two of them became instant soul brothers. They blabbed about pens and pencils way longer than any two people ever have on the face of this planet.

The best part of the night was when Papa Pete came over, because he brought a fresh batch of his garlic dill pickles. That is our favorite snack in the whole world. Papa Pete and I always go out on our balcony and munch on pickles as we watch the moon come up and move across the New York City sky. Trust me, life in my city doesn't get any better than that.

"Would you gentlemen like to join us on the balcony for a pickle?" Papa Pete asked Yoshi and his dad, after my friends had left to go back to their apartments.

"It is my honor," said Mr. Morimoto, bowing.

"Mine, too, *ojiisan*," Yoshi said.

We climbed out onto the balcony. It was a perfect spring night, just cold enough to make your nose turn red. You could smell the city—a little bit of pizza, a little bit of city traffic, and a dash of roasted peanuts.

Papa Pete reached into the plastic bag, pulled out a nice crunchy pickle, and handed it to Mr. Morimoto, using a piece of waxed paper the way we do at our deli.

"Enjoy," he said.

"My teacher said you wouldn't like these," I told Mr. Morimoto.

"Your teacher doesn't like Mexican food,

either," Mr. Morimoto answered.

As he took his first bite of the pickle, it snapped off and crunched between his teeth. That's how you can tell when they're really fresh.

"And here's one for my new grandkid," Papa Pete said, giving Yoshi a pickle and a pinch on the cheek at the same time.

Snap! The pickle crunched between his teeth, too, as he bit into it.

Papa Pete and I reached into the bag and each grabbed a pickle for ourselves.

"These are delicious," Mr. Morimoto said. "I see where Hank gets his ability to cook."

"So the enchiladas turned out good?" Papa Pete asked.

"Very, very good," said Mr. Morimoto.

"Did they have enough zing?" Papa Pete asked.

"Oh, more than enough," I answered.

Yoshi smiled at me. We both knew we were going to remember those enchiladas for a long time.

Then we were quiet. Just the four of us crunching away, watching the moon come up low and orange in the New York City sky.

CHAPTER 25

I DON'T MIND TELLING YOU, it was hard to say good-bye. I had only known Yoshi and his dad for two days, but by the time they left, it felt like we were old friends.

Yoshi promised to write letters. I told him I wasn't so good at letter writing, but I would send videos.

The next day at school, Mr. Morimoto came up to me just before they got in the car to take them to the airport. He bowed, then reached out and shook my hand.

"I must congratulate you, Hank," he said. "You are a fine host. And you are a real chef, too."

"Not really, sir," I answered. "I have to be honest with you about the enchiladas." I couldn't hold it in any longer. "The recipe was too difficult for me to follow because I have trouble with reading. I have what they call *dyslexia*."

It didn't feel so bad telling him the truth now. In fact, it felt good.

"A real chef cooks from his heart," he said, "not from a recipe. In truth, the best things come from the heart, Hank."

Then he bowed once more, waved good-bye to Frankie, Robert, Emily, Ashley—actually to the whole school—and they were on the way home.

All day long I thought about what Mr. Morimoto had said. I heard his words in my head. He thought I was a real chef. Wow. That felt good.

And you know what? I was glad I hadn't stuck to the recipe after all. I came up with my own recipe, my own way to do things. And look what happened. We made a killer batch of a little spicy, but really tasty, one-of-a-kind enchiladas.

Maybe it's not so bad having learning differences after all.

CHAPTER 26

A RECIPE FOR HANK'S ZINGY (BUT NOT TOO ZINGY) ONE-OF-A-KIND KILLER ENCHILADAS

This recipe serves eight people. I make it for Frankie and Ashley all the time now. Make it for your friends. And remember: Great chefs cook with their hearts, so feel free to add your own creative touches. Let me know what you come up with.

Ingredients:

2 cups of tomato sauce

1 tablespoon chili powder *(for zing)*

¼ teaspoon oregano

¼ teaspoon garlic powder

¼ teaspoon cumin *(This stuff is really strong, so be careful!)*

¼ teaspoon salt

3 cups shredded cheddar cheese, or a blend of Mexican cheeses

⅓ cup chopped onion *(Let your mom or dad knock these out.)*

16 small corn tortillas

Instructions:

In a saucepan, combine the tomato sauce, chili powder, oregano, garlic powder, cumin, and salt. Go get an adult to help you turn on the stove to medium heat. (Remember to get an adult to help you. Take it from me: You don't want to burn yourself, inside your mouth or out. That is no fun.)

Cook the sauce until it comes to a boil, then turn the heat down low and let it cook uncovered for 15 minutes. Stir it every once in a while.

Meanwhile, in a small bowl, mix 2 1/2 cups of cheese with the onions.

Warm the tortillas in the microwave, then dip them into the tomato sauce mixture. Lay them in a greased 9-by-13-inch casserole dish.

Fill each tortilla with the cheese-and-onion stuff. Roll it up. Keep filling and rolling until the dish is full.

Sprinkle the leftover tomato sauce and cheese on top.

Go get a grown-up to turn the oven on to 350 degrees. Let it warm up for a few minutes. While it's warming up, you might want to bounce a ball or read this book again.

Put the whole pan in the oven. Bake it for about 25 minutes or until the cheese is melted and bubbly.

Eat your enchiladas and feel very proud of yourself. You just cooked a great meal.

~~Love,~~ Knock your socks off!

Hank

About the Authors

HENRY WINKLER is an actor, producer, and director and he speaks publicly all over the world. Holy mackerel! No wonder he needs a nap. He lives in Los Angeles with his wife, Stacey. They have three children named Jed, Zoe, and Max and two dogs named Monty and Charlotte. If you gave him one word to describe how he feels about this book, he would say, "Proud."

If you gave him two words, he would say, "I am so happy that I got a chance to write this book with Lin and I really hope you enjoy it." That's twenty-two words, but hey, he's got learning challenges.

LIN OLIVER is a writer and producer of movies, books and television series for children and families. She has created over one hundred episodes of television, four movies and seven books. She lives in Los Angeles with her husband, Alan. They have three sons named Theo, Ollie, and Cole, one fluffy dog named Annie, and no iguanas.

If you gave her two words to describe this book, she would say "funny and compassionate." If you asked her what compassionate meant, she would say "full of kindness." She would not make you look it up in the dictionary.